Henry Holl

The Golden Bait

A Novel. Vol. III

Henry Holl

The Golden Bait
A Novel. Vol. III

ISBN/EAN: 9783337003449

Printed in Europe, USA, Canada, Australia, Japan

Cover: Foto ©Andreas Hilbeck / pixelio.de

More available books at **www.hansebooks.com**

THE GOLDEN BAIT.

A Novel.

By HENRY HOLL,

AUTHOR OF

"THE KING'S MAIL," "THE OLD HOUSE IN CROSBY SQUARE,"
"MORE SECRETS THAN ONE," "THE WHITE FAVOUR,"
ETC. ETC.

IN THREE VOLUMES.
VOL. III.

LONDON:
TINSLEY BROTHERS, 18, CATHERINE STREET, STRAND.
1871.

CONTENTS

OF

THE THIRD VOLUME.

THE GOLDEN BAIT.

CHAPTER I.

THE SON OF HIS MOTHER.

THERE is no saying how fast a long stage-coach may be made to go when the coachman has made up his mind to come in handsome, and get over the last part of his journey at a very different rate from what he began it; to rattle over the stones, and show his skill in twisting round difficult corners, and to touch up his horses and put them into a gallop, by way of convincing the inhabitants of whatever town he may happen to drive into that that is his usual pace, that his horses never go at a less speed, and that such a thing as a breakdown upon the road is next to impossible.

Flaring through the dismal outskirts of the town, the coach-lamps first are seen, shining on gable-ends, on low-roofed cottages, on barns, on pigsties, and on deep-thatched outhouses; blinking the glimmer in latticed windows, and blinding

them with double darkness the moment they are
gone; leaving the coach to rattle through the
ill-paved suburb, shaking the windows both of
coach and houses, until it gets into the second
principal street of the town, when the guard
blows his horn, and the whole of the High Street
turns out to receive it as a matter of course.

Now, townspeople, as a rule, are quite as fond
of seeing the coach come in in style, as the coachman is of driving it in style; and if any town
had reason to be proud of its coach, Newark
had, though it only changed horses there, and
went away to rumble through the whole of the
night, and half the following day, until it got to
Berwick. That made no difference. The coach
was their coach; it was always spoken of as
" our coach," and as a matter of principle the
townsfolk stood up for it, and would not permit
a word to be said against it on any terms. And
there it was drawn up at the " Castle"—the
fastest long-stage coach in England, the best-
horsed coach, and a coach as little liable to
accidents as any coach that was ever built.

Mrs. Savaker stood at the door of the " Castle"
to give it the customary welcome, and having
nodded to the coachman, and been nodded to in
return, she set about looking after the customers.
But as they consisted chiefly of townspeople, or

travellers going north, a glass of brandy-and-water
and a warm over the fire were the things most
in request, or a hasty mouthful, and then away
again.

But this time Mrs. Savaker was in luck, for a
gentleman getting out of the coach wished to
know if he could be accommodated with a bed
and have something hot for supper.

The gentleman walked in, and was being
carried off somewhere in charge of the chambermaid, when seeing the little bar-parlour close at
hand, and Mrs. Savaker sitting in it, he asked
if there would be any objection to his taking his
meal in there, as the place looked warm and
comfortable, and he should prefer it, if it made
no difference.

"There's no reason agin' it an' ye like it,"
said Mrs. Savaker, answering the inquiry in
person, "an' can tack things in the rough, an'
no' object to a pipe being smoked by regular
customers to the 'Cas'le.'"

"Anything to be permitted the honour of
your agreeable company," replied the gentleman,
tugging at his great-coat to get it off.

"Eh, you're no half a dab at that. Here,
just give me ain of the sleeves, an' thar', you're
out of your shell you see in no time."

Before he well knew where he was, his coat

was hung up on a peg, his hat on the coat, and a chair set for him in the front of a roaring fire.

"An' noo what will you ha' for supper?" asked the landlady.

"Why, for the matter of that, I am not particular so long as it's hot and soon got ready. That horrible long-stage coach is enough to cramp one for the rest of one's life, and numb one's limbs like a ten weeks' frost."

"Eh, it's no' so bad as that. A coach is a coach, an' the Highflyer not ain of the worst as could be named. It's reckoned a gude un', an' keeps time like an' eight-day clock."

"Maybe. But an eight-day clock wants winding up, and if the Highflyer underwent a similar process now and then, it might start its wheels afresh, and possibly accelerate its speed. I have, however, the greatest regard to its reputation, and will do my best to think as little harm of it as I can, since you seem to take an interest in its rather slow proceedings."

"Oh, it's no' that I care a snap of the fingers about it a'ter it's gone fra' here. Ayent Newark, it may do what it likes, an' crawl like a caterpillar. It's no affair o' mine what it does then, nor's like to be; nor of yours either, I should think, now you've a gude fire to warm at, an' a supper to eat, if you'll only say what it's to be."

" Anything—poached eggs and a toast—a rasher of ham—anything that's handy and soon cooked. In the meantime favour me with a glass of brandy-and-water to drink to the High-flyer, and wish the proprietor and its friends long life and happiness. You see I bear no malice. I am nearly thawed, and by the time I have swallowed the brandy-and-water, I have no doubt I shall entertain a lively appreciation of its coachman, and be anxious to blow a flourish on the guard's horn in honour of its enterprising proprietor."

As Mrs. Savaker did not quite relish her customer's bantering, she tossed her head, mixed the brandy-and-water, and after placing the glass on the table without a word, flung out of the room to give directions about supper.

Left to himself, and in undisturbed possession of that little bar-parlour, the white-headed gentleman eyed about him, and appeared to be mentally reflecting on what he saw. He had observed the landlady quite as attentively, and though he contrived not to let her notice it, had glimpsed his sharp and twinkling eyes at her in a way that Mrs. Savaker would not have liked had she seen him, as she stood mixing the brandy-and-water, and listening to his talk about the coach.

It was a long time since he had seen her—
many long years ago ; and had he not been told
by the north countryman that Poll Woodruff was
the mistress of the " Castle" at Newark, the
chances were he would not have remembered a
line in her face, or thought of her, except by
accident.

And there hung the portrait of the late proprietor of that charming piece of widowhood
over the fireplace : the gentleman to whom she
had been chiefly indebted for her altered condition, and to whose death she owed her present
enviable position of landlady of the " Castle."

He had known Poll of old ; the exciseman he
had not had the happiness to be acquainted
with. But the exciseman seemed to know him,
and to have taken a sudden liking to him, for
he stared at him out of his big saucer eyes, shook
his fat face at him, and twisting the corner of
his mouth, appeared to be whispering a word of
caution in his ear respecting his excitable widow,
and to say, that he had better mind what he was
about, if he did not wish to have the house
tumbled about his ears.

Immediately opposite, and as if to remind the
portrait how much it was indebted to their
agency for its redness and its pimples, stood a
pair of gigantic punch-bowls, turned upside

down, and supporting a pair of lesser bowls upon their stands. There were lemons in profusion— lemons in nets, in glasses, and on the shelves; and the whole place was so full of the combined smell of fruit and spirit, it only required a little imagination to fancy that the ex-exciseman was in for a night of it, and the punch-bowls smoking for his especial benefit.

After some time spent in inspecting the bowls and lemons, the bottles full of rum, of shrub, bitters, and brandy, Mr. Blissett (for it was he) resolved to profit by the occasion and pay all necessary attention to the landlady, under favour of the red-faced gentleman over the fireplace, still looking and winking at him, making all kinds of faces at him, as if to warn him not to tempt his better half too far, nor trifle with a temper so fearfully uncertain.

The landlady's return startled Mr. Blissett from his reverie, and set him eyeing the preparations for his meal with interest, when the servant girl, taking off the covers, left him to the enjoyment of his rasher of ham, poached eggs, and fried potatoes.

"It's weel you are no' particular," said Mrs. Savaker, sitting by the fire after her customer had taken his seat, " an' can stay your stomach wi' eggs an' ham. It's better anyhow than sitting in the lang-stage coach, an' trying to stretch your legs, which you can't, inside the Highflyer."

"Capital! the very thing I like!" said Mr. Blissett, cutting a piece of ham. "As you say, this is better than sitting inside that misnamed vehicle, which I have no hesitation in pronouncing a 'do,' and the greatest imposition that ever crawled upon four wheels."

"It's no' that the 'Cas'le' is bad off, or the larder bad off either," said Mrs. Savaker, when she saw that it was of no use holding on by the Highflyer any longer. "But just the noo, ye see, a' things are clumpy, for market day ain't till Thursday, an' it 'ed be a waste to keep fillin' when there was no one to fill, an' run the chance of spoiling gude meat by keeping it too lang. An' noo what would you like to drink, yell or brandy?"

"Yell by all means, for yell I suppose means ale, and I should like a draught of home-brewed of all things."

"You'll fin' that pretty gude, I tack it," said Mrs. Savaker, as she drew the ale and put it on the table. "It's reckoned the right sort o' stuff, an' gets a deal o' praise fra' the customers at the 'Cas'le.'"

"You are a fortunate woman," said Mr.

Blissett, " to be so well off, and able to make your friends so comfortable. The ' Castle' seems to be a good sort of a house and well managed, and I have no doubt it is a paying concern. It ought to be, I'm sure, with such an agreeable and good-looking landlady."

He said this in his most affable manner, and with a view to make himself agreeable. But Mrs. Savaker—whether she was overdosed by compliments, or did not care to be told of her good looks—kept on at her needlework and took no notice.

" Might I make so bold to ask," said Mr. Blissett, after finishing his supper, and finding his first shot fail, " who this gentleman with the rather florid face, and brass buttons, may be? I see who the other portrait is meant for, and congratulate the artist on his having made so good a likeness."

" Oh —that," said Mrs. Savaker, jerking her head in the direction of the portrait of the defunct exciseman; " that war my husband, and war thow't a gude likeness. But it's not. It's not half red enough, an' a deal too slinky in the shouls for him."

" Too what?" cried Mr. Blissett, utterly confounded as to what " slinky" could possibly mean.

" Why, skinny, if you want a southern word ;
but down north, we ca' it slinky."

· " Infinitely indebted and obliged.   Let it be
slinky by all means.   But if slinky's thin, what
in the name of fortune is the word for fat !   Now,
I should have thought, judging from the picture,
that the artist—Heaven keep him, and preserve
him to the north !—had strained a point to
round him up, and had rather exaggerated than
reduced his size."

" He was no so nice as a' that come te,' an'
ma' be, had a hint given him by the master not
to mack his pictur too fine and dandy-like.   Not
that he was much of a beauty at the best of times,
that I can tell ye, an' say it noo for sartin."

" Then Mr. Savaker, by your admission, was
not so perfect an Adonis as his picture would
lead us to suppose ?"

· " Eh ? you're talking south noo, I suppose,
an' what your glavering means I neither ken nor
care."

" Pardon me.   I was paying the highest compliment to the original of that picture I could
possibly suggest."

" Then you might as weel ha' spared yoursel
the pains, for he no deserved it, but was no
better nor a trough, wi' the tap always running,
an' yet never full."

" Hum," thought the lawyer, " the navigation is difficult, and the ordinary course of sounding the depth of a widow's affection slightly irregular. It is to be regretted," he resumed, " that so admirable a relict as yourself should not have a more praiseworthy object on which to bestow your recollection, and excite your memory to veneration and respect."

" As to a relic," said Mrs. Savaker, rather angrily, " I'm no Papist, nor wor him neither; though he is so smart and braw. So you may as well keep your soft sawder for some one as wants it, an' don't know which side his brede is buttered."

" You utterly and entirely misapprehend my meaning," protested the lawyer, seeing that Mrs. Savaker's religious scruples were likely to be scandalized by the mention of a relict, and that she was about to bounce out of the room. " I earnestly assure you of my personal objection to Pope and Popery, and am too good a Protestant to wish to shock you by any interference with your conscientious expression of belief."

" Weel," said Mrs. Savaker, laying down her work and stirring the fire as if to burn the Pope and all his followers in the blaze, " what is it ye mean? What has a relic to do with him or me, I should like to know; an' hoo comes that

pictur to bounce you like a cracker on Guy
Faulks' night, an' set you talking of what you
no understand?"

"Simply this," replied the lawyer, twisting
round his chair, and bringing himself opposite
the excited but still handsome face of Mrs.
Savaker: " I was anxious to know the state of
your feelings towards that rather red-faced
gentleman, and whether his virtues and his
amiability had entirely obliterated your regard
to his predecessor—if I may be allowed the
word."

" Anan," said Mrs. Savaker, " it's no by a
bubble an' squeak like that I can mack out what
you mean."

" Then this I mean.   Does that grog-blos-
somed likeness of your recent husband at all
resemble your first espoused ?   Or, in plainer
language, does Mr. Savaker remind you in any
way of your first husband, whom you once upon
a time declared to be a lazy, idle vagabond, and
fit for nothing but a rope."

It was Mrs. Savaker's turn to twist about and
stare at her customer, as with her hands on her
knees and her work laid on her lap, she looked
up in his face and tried to remember where she
had seen him.

Failing in this, she fell back on her usual

sullenness, and, scarcely appearing to notice him, replied by a question, instead of by an answer, then bringing down her elbow on the table, she leant on her hand, and said—

" An' what do ye mean by axing that, I should like to know ?"

" This, and this only. That since your first husband deserted you (as you once said he did), how came you to take up with a second, and run a second chance of ill-usage and neglect ?"

Still Mrs. Savaker did not reply. Fixing her eyes on his, she appeared to be trying to recollect where she had seen him, and under what circumstances.

" It is now one-and-twenty years ago—quite one-and-twenty years," said Mr. Blissett, facing the landlady, and looking at her quite as closely as she looked at him; " that having business at Alnwick, I took my wife with me, thinking she might enjoy the trip, and so combine business with pleasure."

" Oh !" said Mrs. Savaker, " I think I ken you noo."

" Well, we went to Alnwick, where I transacted my business, and my wife amused herself in the ordinary way. We had been married nearly three years, but had had no child, and if I may be permitted saying so, there was no sign of one.

My wife was disappointed—I was disappointed—
but as it could not be helped, we made up our
minds to live in hopes, and trust to a prolific
future to make good our loss.   We were capital
walkers in those days, and as my business left
me a good deal of liberty, my wife and I used to
take jaunts into the country, to see the few
sights the neighbourhood boasted.   One day, as
we were returning from a tolerably long walk,
chatting and laughing, or admiring the country,
we were alarmed by hearing a child shrieking
and crying, and calling out as if in terror or in
pain."

"Ah!" said Mrs. Savaker, "I remember it
noo, an' can see it te', as plainly as if it war
before my face."

"Off ran my wife—for, woman-like, she could
not hear a child cry without seeing what was the
matter—and I after her, and soon came up with
the cause of our alarm—a poor miserable child,
lying full length in the road, and its brutal
mother using it most scandalously."

Mrs. Savaker said nothing; but she looked
doggedly before her, and did not appear too well
pleased with the description given of her.

"My wife—and it is only justice to say she
was the first to arrive upon the scene of action—
snatched up the child, faced the woman, and

began to lecture her on her unnatural conduct in a way that ought to have made her thoroughly ashamed of herself; but I regret to say, did not, for beginning to storm and bully, she thought to frighten my splendid little wife, but was mistaken; for of all the brave little women ever lived, my wife is the bravest, and, according to dramatic language, was resolved to save, or perish in the attempt !

"Fortunately for all parties, I arrived just in the nick of time. The woman was about to renew her violence ; and on questioning her, I found that she had been deserted by her husband, and left in the most miserable condition possible. You will perhaps, excuse my frankness, when I say that at that particular moment I was not so much surprised as I ought to have been, but thought he had acted like a prudent man, and pitied the poor fellow from the bottom of my heart.

"But here my wife stepped in. Next to a child being beaten, the thought of a husband running away from his wife, struck her as being cruel and unnatural. She was about to say so, when the woman blazed out in such a towering passion, called him by every name she could lay her tongue to, and conducted herself so intemperately, that my tender-hearted wife began to think as I did, that though her husband might be a brute,

his wife was not an angel, and that after all he
might not be so much to blame as she was."

"Oh, you did, did you?" cried Mrs. Savaker,
with an angry flash of her dark eyes.

"I did, and on telling her what I thought, I
got for my pains as perfect a torrent of abuse as
I ever encountered in my life. There was no
arguing with her; no reasoning; and on our
trying to protect the child, she caught it in her
arms, and would have dashed it on the ground,
had we not prevented her."

Whether Mrs. Savaker half expected to see
that child leap out of the fire, or its little legs
peep down the chimney and crawl into her lap,
Mr. Blissett could not tell. But she looked so
long and earnestly into the fire, it struck him that
she might have some such notion in her mind,
but did not care to say so.

"To leave that child at the mercy of its unnatural mother, could not be thought of for a
moment. It clung to my wife, hid its face
under her shawl, and made such an outcry if the
woman even looked at it, it occurred to me, that
if she would only consent to part with it we might
relieve her of a trouble, supply our own want,
and save the poor little mortal a life of misery
if it continued in the charge of its amiable
parent."

" It was better off, perhaps," said Mrs. Savaker, speaking at the fire, and looking at it earnestly.

" Infinitely better—that is, if you will allow me to be frank, and speak my mind. It may also be gratifying to you to know, that as our adopted son, that boy is now a promising young man, and as profoundly ignorant of everything relating to yourself as if he had never had the happiness of being born your son."

" Ay, ay. It's like enew he ma' be."

" It was a fortunate thing for all of us. We wanted a child; you did not; and as my wife had set her heart on a boy—poor soul !—why here was one ready weaned, and with all his teeth cut. It could not have been better, and as you did not want to keep him——"

" You offered to bring him up and treat him as your awn."

" On your undertaking to give up all claim to him, and leave us at liberty to do with him as we pleased. That matter was soon arranged. You signed your name to the agreement, or rather you put your mark, and the transfer was properly made. It was odd : it certainly was odd, but no sooner had we adopted a child, than we had a chance of one of our own ; and though it arrived rather late, it was not the less welcome because of that, and, what was more, it did not put the poor little fellow's nose out of joint, as might have been expected."

" An' don't he know, then, who are his nataral relations ?"

" Not a word of it. He is as much a part of us as if he were our own ; so much so, I can't help thinking sometimes that we have made a mistake, and that instead of his being our adopted son he came in the regular course of nature, and has as much right to call my wife his mother as his sisters or any other child truly and lawfully begotten."

" An' hoo do you ca' him ?"

" Leonard. I hope you have no objection to the name. It is perhaps only fair to tell you that, whether you object or not, it will make no difference, since we quite intend to stick to the letter of the agreement and call him by whatever name we think proper."

" Belikely enow, an' I'm not going to say anything agin it. But hoo—an' you'll excuse my axing—hoo comes it you ha' come so far by the lang-stage coach to fin' me out ? an' who, I should like to kna', told you I war landlady of the ' Cas'le ' an' wider of that April gowk yonder as hangs over the fireplace ?"

This was a poser. He had not expected to be cross-questioned, and Mr. Blissett stammered and hemmed, looked at the ceiling, then at Mrs. Savaker, until he made up his mind to make a clean breast of it and make her as wise as himself, which after all was not saying much.

"Your question," said Mr. Blissett, "simple as it appears, is not so easy to answer as you may imagine. I will, however, deal fairly by you, and let you know exactly why I trusted myself inside that miserable vehicle and came to Newark to find you out."

"It's an ill wind blaws nabody gude, an' the 'Cas'le' will be a' the better for a bed an' a supper anyhoo."

"Pray include a breakfast and another glass of brandy-and-water. Thank you, and now I will let you know—as much as I know myself; and the reason why I came to see you, to satisfy myself that you were the person the fellow represented, and not somebody else invented to impose upon me."

"Feller! What feller?"

"Well, I don't know exactly how to describe him, except by saying that he thinks himself remarkably clever, and flatters himself he has found out something to make a little money by. He comes from the Border; wears a drab great-coat and a Glengarry cap, and is for ever talking of losing his brass, till I wish he hadn't a penny

2—2

left to lose, or had broken his shins before he ventured on my doorstep and favoured me by daily
calls till I was sick of his very sight."

" Eigh ?" cried Mrs. Savaker, roused out of
her moodiness by the mention of the Glengarry
cap and drab great-coat ; " I know who you
mean weel enow.   A lang-legged chiel as brags,
an' bounces, an' comes looking in at your door
as if he'd steal the flick of bacon hanging ahint
it.   Oh, he's a ketty feller that, an' wanted to
stuff an' cram at my expense, only I would no'
stand it, but sent him away empty as a bagpipe."

" I have no doubt his behaviour justified his
reception, which appears not to have been very
warm.   The first time I had the honour of
meeting him I was bidding a lady and gentleman
good-bye, when I observed this fellow swaggering
up the inn, and staring in at the office doors,
stop, and come to a dead halt at my door-
step."

" But what—what did he want wi' ye ?
Come to that.   I know what he wanted wi' me
weel enow, only I war too many for him, an' let
him know I war not to be dashed by a clever
clumsy chap like he war."

" His first attempt to be agreeable was to
claim acquaintance with the lady—a client of
mine, who happened to be leaving my office in

company with a military gentleman at the time
he came up—much to her annoyance, I might
almost say disgust."

"No, did he though! Haw! haw! haw! I'll
bet a guinea tae a shilling it war the leddy as
slept double wi' the hoose wench, an' the Captain she war afeared on, or pretended to be, to
mack believe she war a chany saucer—no to be
touched except on Sundays."

"I cannot enter into a discussion of that sort,
as I entertain the highest opinion of the lady's
prudence and the gentleman's honour. It was
vexatious enough to have him annoying my client
at my very door without being startled by his
mentioning your name, which I remembered to
have heard at the time you put your mark to the
agreement when you parted with your son."

"No, did he though? I wish I had been
there! I'd ha' doused his chops for un, an'
made 'em smart for being over-familiar wi' his
betters."

"I am happy to say you were not. Had you
by any misfortune met, your united burrs would
have destroyed my sense of hearing for a month
and taken the polish off my furniture. It was
quite bad enough as it was, but as I saw he
wished to speak with me, I thought the best thing
I could do would be to beckon him inside and take

him up to my room and hear what he had to say in private."

" That's what I want to knaw; what *did* he say, and what did he want poking his nose in a gentleman's hoose, as he tried to poke it in the ' Cas'le.' "

" There's the confounding part of it. He said a good deal, and yet said nothing ; spoke of some secret, and of some newspáper he had seen, in which an advertisement had appeared offering a reward for the discovery of some one whose relations he fancied he had found ; kept dinning your name into my ears, nodded and winked, and evidently wished me to understand that he had discovered something which had reference to you and the child I and my wife found you so amiably correcting."

" He did, did he ? A land-louping ne'er-do-weel !"

" He was certainly aware of your having parted with your child to me, though by what means I cannot possibly imagine, and wished to obtain such information as he thought I could supply him with ; but not being disposed to satisfy my gentleman, I saw that he was at his wit's end, and at a loss how to proceed."

" Sarve him right, sarve him right ! It's no to such as him I'd tell a ha'porth of the truth, though I war cut in pieces for it."

"You will understand that, for Leonard's sake, I wish to keep this fellow in ignorance of the facts of the case, or he might otherwise inform him of his parentage, and break his heart by telling him the truth. I have, therefore, determined to keep my own counsel, and turn a deaf ear to his inquiries, fearing lest an indiscretion on my part might give him a clue, and help him in what he wants to know."

"Help him til the gallows, I say! Gie him a leg up, an' leave him kicking at the end of a rape."

"He has evidently found out something, and, having traced that something up to you, talks of making money out of it if he can only get further information, and speaks incessantly of a son of yours having been turned over to the care of a kind-hearted 'boddy' in the north, but who afterwards went abroad. Now this bothers me. *I* am not a kind-hearted 'boddy,' therefore it can't be Leonard. *He* never went abroad, was never in the north, and yet I can't help thinking that he must refer to him, unless you are aware of anything to the contrary, and can set me right."

"I'm not a la'yer," said Mrs. Savaker, darning a hole in a stocking, and seemingly intent upon her work.

"But you are a sharp, clever woman, and as

you are principally interested in this fellow's inquiries, and I think willing to assist me for the sake of your son, I wish particularly to know if you are acquainted with anything that can be of service in this matter, and open my eyes as to what this fellow means, so that I may be able to give him his answer and get rid of him the next time he comes pulling at my office bell."

" An war' it for this you cam' all the way fra Lonnon ?"

" Precisely."

" It's no so easy to come at what you want, sin' this jabbering chap has ta'en it in his hed to meddle an' mack wi' what's no business o' his. The lad's my awn lad. That I will swear te. And though I should no so much mind tacking a squint at him through a winder or a door, somehow or other I dinna want te see him closer, or come anigh him noo the time's lang bye an' gone when he war a babby, an' I war his mither. It's no that I'm unnat'ral, but absence is absence, an' so you see it's better as it is, an' thar's an end o' that."

Mrs. Savaker said this with a tone of feeling strangely at variance with her usual harshness. Yet had she yielded to her natural impulse, she might have expressed herself in terms better becoming her as a mother and a woman. She was hard and stubborn, and, as if determined to prove her indifference to all human sensibility, said what she had to say, and then worked on in silence.

"And is this all you have to tell me? This the entire of your communication after the pains I have taken to risk my neck, and come down here in hopes to gain your confidence? This fellow is no fool, he has spent a considerable sum of money; and, I need scarcely say, that a north countryman would not spend his money unless he saw a chance of making something by it."

"Spent his money, has he?" cried Mrs. Savaker, suddenly excited by the mention of the Northumbrian. "It's more nor he did at the 'Cas'le.' Let him spend, an' may the deil flay me gin I wouldna roast an' burn afore I'd say a word to help him."

"Oh, then you could say something if you would?"

"Naething as wud be a use to him, an' naething as wud mack you worse nor better nor you are, nor do the lad a gude. It's no a thing I had to say I'd say to put that feller right, though you pulled my tongue out an' cut it into collops."

Mrs. Savaker was wroth, Mrs. Savaker was

indignant, and, rightly judging that the more
you try to persuade a woman she is wrong the
more she will insist she is right, Mr. Blissett
gave over further intercession. He was satisfied
by her vehemence that Leonard had no connec-
tion with the Northumbrian's inquiry, and was,
therefore, contented with his journey; and
further thought that though Poll Woodruff was,
in a worldly sense, improved, yet as Mrs. Savaker
she still possessed the quickness of temper which
in former years had distinguished her, when she
flung her child down in the road, and could with
difficulty be prevented using it still worse.

"All I can say is," Mr. Blissett murmured,
as he went upstairs to bed, "I would advise my
friend in the Glengarry cap to keep at a
respectful distance, and not come within reach
of a poker with Mrs. Savaker sitting by it. As
sure as he has a head upon his shoulders the
poker will be flung at it, and, if it hits, adieu to
his hopes of 'brass' and a five hundred per cent.
return on his expenditure."

Mrs. Savaker still sat—sat with her elbows on
her knees, and her face resting on her hands.
The Northumbrian and his bread and cheese rose
in her throat and choked her, whilst his Glengarry cap appeared to be peeping in at her snug
bar-parlour, and his big, staring eyes taking

notes of all he saw ! of herself and of her supper,
and of the late lamented Savaker mounted over
the fireplace as the safest place he could find.

Mrs. Savaker was low-spirited. But as it was
necessary to rouse herself, she mixed herself a
glass of something warm, and then returned to
sit and think, and watch the fire fading in the
grate.

But as she passed the door by which Mr.
Blissett had left the room, she stood and paused,.
looked over the red blind, and watching him as he
went upstairs to bed, she whispered to herself—

"Eigh, but you're wrang for aince. You're
no so canny but you've made a blunder, an'
la'yer though ye be, ain't clever enou' to find out
what ye want. The other chap war close an'
close, an' might ha' found out what he axed for
(not that I knaw the gude o' it) had he no' been
so grippy an' so great a shabrag as he war. It's
agin a stane wall ye split your heds, an' knaws
a naething o' what ye wants te knaw. I ken
what 'tis that bothers ye, an' hoo a word would
set ye right—provided that ain or baith could
be made better for it, an' Poll Savaker see her
way to what war to come of it."

CHAPTER II.

UNEXPECTED MEETINGS.

THE following day was not ushered in by one of Mrs. Savaker's good-tempered mornings. She got out of bed the wrong side, and was in about as savage and ill-conditioned a humour as any landlady well could be. The bar-parlour was no longer enlivened by her agreeable company, nor her customer favoured with another sight of her before the coach came thundering up the street; when an equally complimentary coachman with the one belonging to the Highflyer rattled the Tally-ho to the door of the "Castle," and made believe as though a dozen miles or more made no difference to him or to the horses, nor indeed to anything belonging to the Tally-ho.

Dissatisfied with the result of his journey, dissatisfied with Mrs. Savaker, and out of patience with all and everything belonging to the "Castle," Mr. Blissett paid his bill, shook himself in a corner of the coach, and settled it in his mind that from that time forth he would forget that such a person as Poll Woodruff had ever lived, or that such a burry gentleman as the

north countryman had ever halted on his door-
step and led him to think that some mystery was
associated with his adopted son, through his
shrugs, his winkings, his humming, and his
hawing.

Scarcely had he buried himself in his corner,
and before the coach had turned into the second
best street in the town, when he saw, running up a
cross street, and shouting at the top of his voice,
the ubiquitous north countryman coming at full
speed, yelling and calling and waving his cap to
the coach to stop.

Unwilling to be cut short in a most tre-
mendous gallop, but more unwilling to lose a
passenger, the coachman made as though he had
the greatest difficulty in reining in the horses,
and when at last he succeeded, and the burly
figure of the Northumbrian came puffing and
blowing to the side of the coach, Mr. Blissett
could hardly trust his eyesight until he heard his
well-known voice call out—

"Canna ye wait for a mon when ye see him
running, an' hear him ca' or wave his bonnet?
Passengers are no so plenty by the lang stage I
shu'd think, but you might wait to pick one up,
an' not gie him the trouble to blaw himsel out
like a bladder to put brass into your pocket."

Whatever reply the coachman grunted through

his muffler was inaudible. The Northumbrian climbed outside and sat himself on the extreme end of the seat in front of the coach, and as he sat on his side, Mr. Blissett could see his long drab skirts flap over the rail as he pleasantly enlivened that side of the coach by the full view of his spatterdashes.

"Now if that is not the most vexatious individual," said Mr. Blissett, leaning out of the window and feeling strangely tempted to pull at the coat-tails, " I never had the misfortune to encounter one! Go where I will, do what I will, he is sure to be there, and I verily believe if I were on the top of the Monument, or at the bottom of a well, I should see him skimming in the air, or sticking in the mud."

As leaning out of the window slightly discommoded his opposite neighbour, and as the gentleman complained of a through draught, and of a head and shoulders interfering with his view, Mr. Blissett drew back, pulled up the glass, and inwardly protested his objection to the Northumbrian, whose coat-tails flapped and flapped, beat against the window, or spread and streamed across, while his Glengarry cap, reflected in the road, appeared at every lurch of the coach to be making bobs at him and bowing to him as if to inform him that he knew he was inside, and what he was doing.

The gentleman in the opposite corner did not promise to be a very lively companion, for he kept nodding his head, woke up with a jerk, and stretched and yawned as though he had not been in bed all night.

This was all very well for a time, but it became at last so troublesome that Mr. Blissett lost patience; protested against his neighbour's legs sprawling over on his side, and told·him of it rather smartly. But as the other took no notice, he kicked his legs out of the way, shook ·him, and made him understand that he was not lying full length in bed, but sitting in a coach, where there was hardly room to sit, much less to stretch.

The gentleman apologized. Mr. Blissett was pacified, and beginning to talk, tried to engage him in conversation; but, finding this rather slow, and that his companion looked as if he were going off to sleep at the least pause, he changed his tactics, pointed out the different objects on the road, praised the beauty of the country, and, in short, did everything that he could to make the gentleman, if not companionable, less like a lay figure stuck up in a corner of the coach than the person he appeared to be.

But as he looked at him he could not help thinking that he had seen him somewhere before, though for the life of him he could not remember where. After trying for some time to recall when he had met him, he jogged him and said—

"You'll excuse me; but I surely have met you before. You are, I perceive by your dress, a clergyman; and as I cannot boast of a very extensive acquaintance with gentlemen of your cloth, I ought to remember you, but don't. Can you enlighten me? or, am I mistaken in my supposition?"

"Oh, no. You are right enough," said the gentleman, with a yawn. "I knew you the instant you got in, but did not say so."

"And where, may I ask, had I the pleasure of seeing you?"

"At a funeral."

"A funeral?"

"Yes; at the funeral of a hard-drinking uncle of mine, who died a month or two ago, and was buried a little way out of town to suit some ridiculous whim or other, and cause us extra trouble, I suppose, in seeing the last of him."

"Of course it was; and here have I been trying and trying to make it out, and could not. Poor Dick! Poor old fellow! And are you his nephew? Of course you are. You are as like your brother as two peas, and I ought to have known you at a glance. But then you see I have a bad memory for faces, and can't for the life of me recollect who's who."

" Not even your clients?"

" No, not even my clients. But that's excusable. Clients never look twice alike. One day they are all life and spirits, the next as dull as ditch-water, according to the state of their affairs. Now, a young handsome fellow like your brother, who has had a slice of luck——"

" You need not remind me of it. The subject is not so agreeable that we need talk about it."

" He, of course," said Mr. Blissett, finishing the sentence, " would look pleased and happy; and I have no doubt that you would look equally pleased under similar circumstances."

" I am not so sure of that. As a clergyman, I hope I know my duty better than to set too great a store by worldly gains."

" Of course, of course. Clergymen, as we know, are notoriously averse to that kind of thing, and rather prefer a modest independence to excessive wealth," said Mr. Blissett, with a half comical glance at his companion.

" It is, I believe, a well established fact, and I only wish my brother (you say you think I am like him) entertained the same opinion, and that he were less mercenary now he has come into possession of so considerable a fortune."

" Well, I must say I have seen no proof of his nearness at present."

" Not ? But we'll not refer to it if you please ; the subject is a painful one, and I would rather not talk of it. As regards our resembling one another, there is of course a family likeness, though I can't help thinking that over-application to theological study may have given my face a certain expression that——"

" I understand ; a more refined expression you mean. The sort of expression the women are so fond of, and run after as if they were mad. You may always know when there is some dear creature of the sort come into a new neighbour- hood by the slippers and braces you see working and mounted ; as if parsons were the only men in the world who wore braces, or could not afford to buy slippers."

" I presume the ladies are the best judges of what they do, and I must leave them to answer you," replied Mr. Ernest, rather grandly.

" ' You shall never take a woman without her answer, unless you take her without her tongue,' says Rosalind. But, as you say, they are the best judges of what they do ; and, though we can't always agree with them, let us at least give them credit for meaning well."

Mr. Blissett bowed by way of compliment. Mr. Ernest did the same, and for a few moments the conversation dropped. Seeing his companion going off to sleep again, the lawyer roused him by saying—

"That uncle of yours was an odd fish, and liked to swim in troubled waters, if we may judge by his career."

"He was an abominably selfish and intemperate person," said Mr. Ernest, evidently speaking his true sentiments, and less on his guard than he had been. "Had he been a gentleman, or even tolerably attentive to his religious duties, he would have at least led a different kind of life, and at his death have left his property in a very different way from what he did."

"Oh, oh," thought Mr. Blissett, "that's where the shoe pinches, is it?"

It was easy to see that the Colonel had not died in that odour of sanctity and goodwill to all men certain of his relatives desired, and that Mr. Ernest Arkwright had some especial ground of complaint, he not having been remembered in his will. The Colonel had forgotten Mr. Ernest. Mr. Ernest was indignant; and, notwithstanding his indifference to money, he did not seem disposed to put up with it quietly.

Once set going upon a subject upon which he could talk, Mr. Ernest Arkwright began by informing Mr. Blissett that, though his uncle, the Colonel, had treated him scandalously, he forgave him, as a Christian ought, and was quite prepared to forget that such a wicked old monster had ever lived; to be content with what he had, and perform a nephew's part to his uncle, the Rector, who had recently appointed him his curate. He had all the work to do, he said, but that, of course, he did not so much mind, as his uncle was getting old, and wanted somebody he could depend upon faithfully to discharge the duties he was called upon to fulfil, whether great or small.

His uncle was far from being well, he said. Indeed, he thought, he was very ill, and could not live another year; he had grown so corpulent he could hardly stir, and his doctor entertained the most unfavourable opinion as to the state of his health; so much so, that he should not be surprised if he died while he was away, but in a different frame of mind, he hoped, to his uncle Richard.

Without exactly wishing for his uncle William's death, Mr. Ernest seemed to entertain a very favourable opinion of his partiality towards himself, and thought it not improbable that as his uncle, the Colonel, had left his fortune to his brother, his uncle the Rector might leave the bulk of his property to him, and make him a suitable return for the attention he had paid him. He would then have an opportunity to show his brother the difference in their dispositions, and convince him, that though he had not even made an offer to share his money with him, he bore no malice, but would make him a liberal allowance at any time he might come to want it.

He had seen nothing of him, so he said, and did not expect to see him, for it was quite evident he wished to withdraw entirely from his family, and hold himself aloof from them, now he had become rich, and thought perhaps that they might require his help. It was, of course, sadly to be regretted that such selfishness should exist in the world, and he was quite certain that his brother had been persuaded to it by that wretched little Methodist, to whom he had been mad enough to engage himself, without the least regard to his (Mr. Ernest's) feelings, or consulting him on so momentous a question as to the difference in their religious opinions.

" But the worst part of all," as he informed Mr. Blissett, " was his want of duty to his

parents.　He had not written to them for up-
wards of six weeks, and they did not even know
what had become of him.　His mother was so
wretched about him, and· his father so anxious,
that they had sent for him (Mr. Ernest) to go at
once to London and make inquiries after him ;
for his father was too ill, and his mother unable
to leave home in consequence.　All this, my good
sir, you will allow, is a great trouble to me, and
a great inconvenience ; still, as my dear brother's
safety is of such vital importance, and superior
to all other considerations, I consented to my
parents' wish, obtained leave from my dear good
uncle, the Rector, and am at this moment on my
road to London, to try and find out the mother
of this girl—whose name, I am informed, is
Rushbrook—to see if my eloquence will have any
weight in persuading her to break off the match,
and accept a sum of money—from my brother,
of course—to prevent her bringing an action
against him for breach of promise."

　" And haven't you heard what has taken place
in that quarter ?"

　" Not a word, though I am sadly· afraid he
has married her, and disgraced me by an alliance
with a family which is base enough to set itself up
in opposition to those most valuable of all in-
stitutions—Church and State.　You may well

stare, sir! You may well look shocked, and I
am sure you will easily imagine what I as a
Churchman feel when I tell you, that I think it
more than probable that he has married this Dissenter, and that it is not impossible that the
money, which by right belongs to us, will be ab-
sorbed by that disreputable connexion, or go in
building meeting-houses, instead of keeping up the
dignity of the National Church."

" The case, as you put it, certainly seems hard,
and I can quite enter into your feelings when
speaking of his money. But as the lady is
already married——"

" Married !" cried the Reverend Mr. Ernest.
" Married !—you don't surely mean to say it ?
Well, of all the disgraceful things I ever heard,
this is the worst. I look upon his behaviour as
unchristian and abominable. I feel myself insulted and disgraced, I consider myself robbed
and plundered of my prospective right to at least
some share of my brother's property, but shall
endeavour to bear with humbleness this new
affliction, and think that the more scandalously
he behaves to me and to his parents, it is my
duty to forget his ingratitude, and forgive him,
though he don't deserve it."

" As I before said," Mr. Blissett resumed, " as
the lady is now married, and not to him——"

"Eh! Not married to him? Is the match
broken off, or has she jilted him, and flung herself into the arms of some wretched Methodist
like herself, and spared us the humiliation of
being connected with a descendant of that old
psalm-singing vagabond, Josiah Hindmarsh? Oh,
my dear sir, you cannot imagine the load you
have taken from my mind; you cannot conceive
the happiness I feel, and the grateful glow that
fills my veins when I reflect that, though Frederick has not behaved himself so well as I could
wish, he is not so lost but he may be reclaimed,
and brought to believe in filial affection and
brotherly regard."

Had Mr. Ernest spoken in the pulpit as well
as he spoke in the coach, there would have been
some hope of him. There was no mistaking
what he meant this time; no hammering and
stammering, and no halting for words. His
matter might be a little loose, but his energy
made amends for all, and assured his hearer that
he was in earnest, and thoroughly acquainted
with his subject.

"Pray spare yourself unnecessary pains to
express your feelings," said Mr. Blissett. "They
are easily understood, and I fully comprehend
the depth of your emotion on hearing that your
brother is still a bachelor, and not likely to do

anything to forfeit your affection by wasting his money."

Mr. Ernest did not quite know what to make of his companion, or if he were quizzing him or not. He thought it better not to be too curious about his meaning, but to accept as a compliment (as many a gentleman has done before), what on investigation might have proved a censure. Passing his cambric handkerchief over his face, he fanned himself slightly, took off his gloves and rubbed up his hair; then asked with an air of perfect contentment,

"Can you tell me the name of the person this girl has married? Some holder-forth on a common I suppose, roaring himself hoarse on the top of a milestone; or some loud mouthed fellow bellowing in a chapel at the end of a blind alley, where his misguided followers go to listen to him, and put halfpence in a wooden bowl. As if such a fellow as that had as good a right to preach as a clergyman who, properly ordained by his bishop, is also qualified by his education to be a minister of the Church."

"Permit me to disabuse your mind. The gentleman you allude to neither roars on a common nor lives by halfpenny contributions. I should say he would prefer a silver dish to a

wooden bowl, and if asked for money, would give
a sovereign and not a copper. He is a gentleman of family and fortune, able to take his wife
into the best society, and certainly has no reason
to be ashamed of anything he does, whether as
a Churchman or a Dissenter."

" I am heartily glad to hear of her good
fortune," said Mr. Ernest, a little less elated than
before, and slightly annoyed at Mr. Blissett's
placing a Low Dissenter on a level with a High
Churchman. " May I venture to ask his name ?"

" Ellerton."

" Ellerton, Ellerton ?" said Mr. Ernest, repeating the name.

" Yes. Mark Ellerton."

" Mark Ellerton. I have certainly heard that
name before, and very recently."

The time required to refresh his memory
having lasted some minutes, Mr. Blissett thought
that he had gone to sleep, and did not care about
disturbing him ; when the coach gave a sudden
bump and startled the reverend gentleman to
his feet, to look out of the window and see what
had happened—at the moment that the north
countryman jumped down from the outside, and
stood swearing and cursing at the coachman in
the middle of the road.

" That's the fellow who told me the name,"

cried Mr. Ernest. " That fellow with the drab coat who kept me in the vestry turning over the leaves of the register till I was nearly frozen. That broad-shouldered fellow standing in the middle of the road and swearing so dreadfully, that if I had time I would certainly have him brought before the Bench under the profane swearing clause or act, or whatever it may happen to be."

" That !" cried Mr. Blissett, looking from the window. " That——"

But at this moment the horses made a sudden plunge, and nearly knocked him backward as they drew the coach still closer on the waggon against which it had originally bumped, and began to kick and plunge most furiously. The waggon itself stood still; but it rose so high above the coach, that it looked as if it would have fallen and crushed it, but for the four broad wheels and the powerful axles that supported it.

The further window was blocked up by it, its big hoops and covering scraping against the side, while the holloaing and shouting in the road were enough to make the horses bolt. It appeared on inquiry that the coach wheels had locked into the waggon wheels, and that though the horses had been backed, it did not

mend matters, but rather made them worse.   So
they tried to back the waggon, and by so doing
dragged the coach back with it on to the
horses, and then there was the devil and all
to pay.

The coachman lashed, the horses plunged;
when down scrambled the rest of the outsides,
and the insides thought of getting out as well.
But at that moment the horses got frightened,
and, dragging and pulling, broke off one of the
wheels, and drew the coach clear of the waggon,
when over it fell with a thundering crash, and
lay broadside on the road.

Away went the horses ; out jumped the Reverend Mr. Arkwright in time to save himself, and
be shaken hands with by the Northumbrian as an
old friend, though he had only seen him once,
and congratulated on his escape.   But on looking
for his companion, he found him stunned and in-
sensible inside the coach—against the side of
which he had been thrown when it fell over—
lying among the broken glass and shattered
framework.

Thus for a second time the long-stage coach
had come to grief, but luckily had only one
passenger injured.   The Northumbrian was safe.
The Reverend Mr. Arkwright was safe ; but Mr.
Blissett was picked out with a broken collar-

bone and a good deal shaken. The hurt was serious for a man of his time of life, but as the accident took place close by an inn upon the road, he was soon got into bed and a doctor sent for, in whose charge we will leave him.

CHAPTER III.

MARGARET'S HOME.

IF Mrs. Rushbrook had formerly had reason to complain of her son-in-law's conduct, and of Margaret's extraordinary silence, she had now a double cause of wonder and complaint. She wrote, but receiving no answer was left in ignorance of her daughter's health, so that at last she determined to visit them and ascertain for herself the true position of affairs, when she received a brief and formal communication from her son-in-law, in which he stated that in consequence of his wife's indisposition he had been advised to take her abroad in hopes that change of air and scene might benefit her and restore her to health.

Had Margaret then been ill? Had she, as her mother, been kept in ignorance of her state, and only at the last informed of it at a time she was in a critical condition and required a change of air and scene to renovate her?

It would not bear thinking of, and notwithstanding her wish to avoid altercation with a man of Ellerton's obstinate disposition, she was roused

to assert her feeling as a mother, and act as she
ought to do whether he liked it or not.

But in the morning, just as she was setting
out, a second letter arrived, in which he spoke
of " his exceeding gratitude for her having selected him to be her daughter's husband, before,
as she was aware, her affection had been trifled
with, or her fancy occupied by some one else."
The letter then went on to say, " that as she
and her daughter had always acted so fairly by
him, so openly, and with so much confidence,
he thought it only proper to be equally candid
with her, and say, that for a year or two they
should remain abroad. That before she received
his letter they should have left for the Continent,
but that he would avail himself of an early opportunity to relieve her anxiety, and would at
all times study to treat her with the same consideration she had treated him."

There was something in the tone of the letter
she did not like. Insinuations delicately hinted,
yet not the less galling because of that! A
distant formal way of saying spiteful things,
inducing her to think that by some means or
other he had discovered her daughter's previous
engagement, and the part she had played in
leading him to think that there was no impedi-
ment to the match.

She was powerless to help! Unable to befriend! As Margaret's husband he could exercise unlimited control, and the first use he made of it was to remove her from her mother and her friends! He had taken her abroad and carried her away without affording her the opportunity of a parting word—a parting tear! He had torn her child from her! In her sickness he had not consulted her, and outraged nature swelled in that mother's breast until it almost maddened her.

And then from blaming him she came to accuse herself. To feel that as a mother she had studied her daughter's peace less than her own advantage, and, that instead of consulting her inclination, she had wilfully sold and bartered her; parted with her in exchange for worldly gain, and like a thing of traffic, had consented to her sale! Retribution now had come upon her. Day or night the same unmitigated sorrow came with recollection of her daughter, while her heart ached with thinking of her.

Could she indeed have seen her, or watched her deprived of reason, she might have accused herself still further, or cursed him with the bitterest curse that ever woman uttered, as the cause of all. She could not pierce the darkness where she lay, nor hear her moans; knew nothing

of her condition or where her husband had immured her, nor of her being incessantly watched
over by the remorseless jailor to whose charge
he had confided her.

It was fortunate that this knowledge was
withheld, and that she knew nothing of her
daughter's real condition. Had she known more
she would have felt the more, and by her interference have increased her daughter's sufferings
instead of relieving them. By exciting her husband's enmity, she might have roused in him a
sense of opposition, and a determination to
show that what he chose to do he would perform, now that he had the power, and would carry
out his peculiar notions of right and wrong, by
adding to the misery of one he thought had injured him.

Too cunning to betray his secret, but determined to exact the fullest retribution on his
guiltless wife, and punish her mother by keeping
her in ignorance of what had happened, he wrote
to tell her of her illness, and of their going
abroad, but told her nothing further. He explained nothing, and did not openly complain,
yet by his doubtful language led her to suppose
that something had occurred to interrupt that
harmony she thought would repay her daughter
for her obedience, and make her, as her mother,

satisfied and contented with the match she had
brought about.

She never thought of asking herself the question whether her son-in-law might be deceiving
her, and imposing on her credulity by inventing
stories of her daughter's absence purposely to
keep her from going to her.   She never thought
of that, nor entertained a doubt that what he
said was true.   Yet had she gone in hopes to
see her daughter, she would have found the
house shut up, the grounds neglected, and no
one left about the place but Angus and the old
cross-tempered housekeeper.   The rest of the
servants had been dismissed.   The gardener and
even Jane were gone !—Jane, the light yet true-
hearted Jane, who in her desire to please her
mistress, and to do a wobegone lover a service,
had been the cause of all this change, of her
own dismissal, and of the gloom and melancholy
that reigned about the place.

This seemed to agree with Angus.   He had
nothing to do now, but could sit or lounge about
just as he pleased.   At times, indeed, he seemed
to long for Jane to be there, and missed her sly,
tormenting ways.   But when he thought of her
treachery—how she had endeavoured to impose
upon his master, and cheat him too, by trying
to introduce a stranger to the house at the very

time he was hiding in the avenue, and saw her come and go upon her treacherous errand—he thought perhaps that she was a good riddance after all, and not worth fretting about.

His chief employments were watching beneath the evergreens, and pacing up and down to prevent anybody going from the house or coming to it. Here, night by night, he took his stand, though often with a deadly paleness on his brow and a quiver of his limbs, when he fancied he heard a sigh steal through the leaves, or thought he saw the stalking figure of some murdered man start out, as if to catch him in his arms and carry him away.

He struggled hard to get rid of these horrid fancies, and to trace to natural causes the sounds he thought he sometimes heard of groans and murmured cries. He even went so far as to laugh one night, as if to mock that sighing groan. But he never tried it after. For on his laugh there came a frightful echo, while a suppressed chorus of unearthly laughter answered in reply, enough to wake the dead.

He came to dread the place at last, and could hardly summon courage to take his stand at night and watch, as his master bid him. There was no sleeping on his post; fear kept him wide awake ! No lounging and no variety to take off

the horror of the place, or lessen the dread he
apprehended that at an unexpected moment some
apparition would start up and terrify him into a
fit of madness.

Even the bill-hook had ceased to be a common
staff with an axe at the top of it; but appeared
to have grown out of all proportion, and become so
unwieldy that he could hardly lift it, or endure to
look at it; for every time he looked it seemed
to remind him of some fearful deed in which he
had been engaged, and then he thought that if
he could only get rid of it he should get rid of
the memory too, and be a new man again.

It made no difference. He felt it on his
shoulder whether he carried it or not; saw its
shadow following him and coming after him
just the same; and then he knew for certain that
it was not so much the weight of the bill-hook, as
his conscience, that made him so afraid and
nervous.

If his master would only let him off watching
that outside room, and set him some other duty,
he would not care. Anything but that! Anything but walking up and down that horrid place,
keeping guard, and protecting it from the fright-
ful-looking things he saw peeping through the
trees, and trying to frighten him away. There
was no change now. No gipsy to look after, and

nothing to do since he and the whole tribe had left the neighbourhood; nothing but that incessant guard-keeping, and the wearying task of seeing that all was safe.

The long-coated stranger, even he was gone! Jane, servants, gardener, all gone but his master and himself and the old housekeeper. They could not very well get on without some woman in the house, or she would have gone as well; but as they must have some one, and as there was less chance of her betraying him than a stranger, or of her saying something which might get him into trouble, why his master had fixed on her.

The whole place had changed, and was not a bit like what it used to be, with all the windows closed and the house shut up; and as for his master, he should not have known him, he was so changed in the last few weeks, and kept walking about as if unable to keep quiet in one place to save his life, but always on his legs, always walking, and looking so gloomy, that Angus felt rather uncomfortable at times about going near him, for he seemed to avoid him now, and turned away with a half shudder when he saw him, instead of meeting him with a smile as he used to do.

But the most curious thing of all was his

watching him and looking after him when he thought he did not see him. He could not surely suspect him, after what he had done, of playing him false. It was hard if he did, and, what was more, Angus did not like it, and felt inclined to say so. But what was he to do? He was wretched enough already without being ill friends with his master, and as he had sworn to be a faithful servant to him, why it was his duty to put up with a little annoyance, and say nothing about it.

But he did not like it for all that, nor the way his master sometimes spoke to him, and threw out hints as if he half suspected he might betray him, or let the people in the neighbourhood know what he was about. He could not bear that. He had risked his life to do him a service, but to be suspected and doubted were worse than all. It made that outside room and all about the evergreens more dull and dark than ever, the blood upon the ground start out afresh, and break through the thin covering of dust and leaves he had scattered over it in hopes to cover it and hide it from his sight.

But did it hide it? Did it wholly blot it out, or smear it over so effectually that he could not see it, or trace it lying close beside those old black stems, and the path that led through them? It might to some one else, but not to him. He saw it day or night. In his dreams or wide awake, it was all the same, and as to walking over it, he would as soon have thought of jumping into his grave as set a foot within a yard of it.

If he had only some one to speak to, he should not so much mind, or if his master were a little more sociable, or the housekeeper less of a spit-fire; but to go on in that way for ever, was too much even for Angus, and he would have given one of his ears if Jane had only conducted her-self properly, and been permitted the run of the house, to make things pleasant and comfortable as they used to be.

Now strange to say, Jane was thinking the same sort of thing herself, and had some thoughts of trying if she could prevail on him to let her go up to the house occasionally, and throw open the windows, if only to let in the air, and make it look a little more lively. Every one was talk-ing of it, and wondering what on earth had hap-pened that Mr. Ellerton should go wandering about the place like a private watchman, and Mrs. Ellerton never by any chance be seen.

If she could only coax Angus to let her in and do as she wished, she could soon manage the rest, and make herself so useful that they would never think of sending her away. Her mother was old,

and so great a martyr to rheumatism, it was a
mercy she managed to hobble about at all, or
look after anything even in the blundering way
she did ; and as to comfort, such a thing was not
to be expected with no one to help, and only her
poor old mother to attend to everything.

If she could only set her foot inside, let them
get it out again if they could ; and as she had
made up her mind to try, the present was as
good a time as any, perhaps the best, and not a
moment was to be lost in case something should
happen to prevent her going there at all.

In the first place she took a little extra pains
to make herself look smart, arranged her hair,
pinned on her bows, then giving a last look in
the glass, flattered himself she should have no
difficulty with Angus, but made as sure of capti-
vating him as she made sure of anything.

Now Jane, although she had been turned
away, had a character to her back, and plenty
of people to espouse her cause. She had been
born in the town, her mother and father had
been born there as well, and it was not so easy
to set people against her as her master thought,
though he had packed her off without her proper
warning, and given positive orders not to let her
into the house again.

But Jane had been bred in the house, and

from her childhood upward had been reckoned as much a part of it as its climbing roses, its honeysuckles, or the daisies on the lawn. Root out as you will, and stub up as you will, wild shoots will grow and daisies spring. And so it proved with Jane. Turn her away, and she came back again; shut the doors on her, she managed to creep in somewhere, and upon the present occasion she thought she should contrive to get a peep at the old place by some means or other, in spite of her late master or his man.

She had another reason apart from her anxiety about her mother's health, but that will come with time. One reason was as good as twenty, and as her present excuse for going to the house was apparently to satisfy herself that her mother was in her usual doubtful state of health, she thought it would answer her purpose as well as the best, and take off suspicion from the real motive of her visit.

Swing went the lodge-gate on its hinges as Jane tripped through it, and kept along towards the house as unconcernedly as if she had a right to go there, and had not been turned away for bad behaviour. There was no one to stop her— no one to tell her to go back, and even if there had been, Jane was not the sort of girl to be turned back without knowing the reason why.

" At all events," she thought, " they cannot
kill me, even if they do find me out ; nor set the
dogs at me, for the dogs wont bite, and ain't so
apt to forget old friends as some people might
wish, and, what's more, wont fly at me I know.
Besides, I have not done anything so very
dreadful after all, and have nothing to be afraid of.
It's much more likely that *they* may have reason
to be afraid of me, and if they don't mind what
they are about they may come to know it too."

As if to prove her words, and let her see that
she was not so soon forgotten as they hoped for, a
huge Newfoundland, and a couple of unwieldy
pups, came barking with delight the moment they
saw her, and made such a fuss with her, it was
as much as she could do to prevent old Nan lick-
ing her face, and the pups tearing her dress, by
way of showing their fondness.

" No fear of the dogs, at least," thought Jane.
" You're not in the habit of forgetting old friends,
are you, Nan ?   Are you, Juno and Pompey ?
Not a bit of it—but I'll trouble you to leave my
face alone, and leave off crumpling me to pieces,
or I shan't be fit to be seen."

What with coaxing and slapping, scolding and
praising, she had enough to do to keep them
down, and prevent them barking their hearts
out.   But the mischief was done.   Angus had

heard them, and coming to see what was the matter, he saw his old sweetheart looking prettier than ever, walking towards the house, and the dogs jumping about her as if they would have eaten her.

"Well, Angus," said Jane, determined not to wait to be questioned, but to make her excuses beforehand, "Here I am, you see, and come to know how mother is after this goodness knows how long. It's not very right of me, I know, to keep so long away, and mother so ill; but you are such odd people here, one hardly likes to come for fear of being found fault with, or not allowed to go into the house, which gracious knows ain't too delightful a place to look at as it is."

"Oh, the house is well enough," said Angus, "and might have been better had you left it alone, and not got the people turned away because of your doing what you oughtn't. It was a bad bit of business that, Jane, and you ought to be ashamed of yourself for what you did."

"There—there—now don't talk nonsense, but tell me about mother. I am dying to know how she is, and what has happened to her since I have been away."

"Oh, she's pretty middling, and not quite so savage as she used to be. Not that there's much difference. But, between you and me, I think it was that gardener fellow who used to set her on to show her spite to me, and make things disagreeable."

"Oh! oh! It's the gardener still, is it?" thought Jane—then in a more conciliatory tone, "Do you know, Angus, I shouldn't wonder if it was, for mother and he were always great friends, and used to try and set me against you too; only it was of no use. I knew you better than that, and always took your part—only you would not try and make yourself amiable, and so you lost your chance."

"I don't know what you call amiable."

"Why, being good-natured, to be sure, and looking pleasant—which those who didn't know you so well as I do, wouldn't say was one of your weaknesses."

"Oh!" said Angus, "that's what being amiable is, is it?"

"Of course—and speaking civilly when you're spoken to. Now, for instance, I don't think your manners are at all amiable at present. You don't answer me kindly, nor treat me as if you wished I should break my heart about you, and give up all thoughts of the gardener, though he has got a new place, and keeps teasing my life out to marry him, only I wont."

"I ain't going to say I think you wrong, when I think you right; for if I was a woman I'd do away with myself before I'd marry such a fellow as that."

"My sentiments exactly, and, if mother can only be coaxed over not to insist on it, why then you know there may be a chance for you and me after all."

"Not if it depends on her."

"I'm not so sure of that. You only.let me get to see her, and have a long talk with her, I think I know a something that may make her change her mind about him."

"It's against orders, Jane; and I'm not allowed to let you see her," said Angus, as if he had some trouble in bringing out his words, and did not quite like refusing anything his sweetheart asked.

"What! not go in to see my mother! Not see her, when she is dying perhaps; and hasn't a soul to look after her! But, I *will* see her. I'll see her this instant, and if you or your master try to prevent me, you'd better look to yourselves, that's all; for, sure as I'm alive, I'll go before the Bench and let the magistrates know what I suspect of your keeping *some one* locked up, to say nothing of mother, who, for aught I know, may be locked up too, and cruelly used as well."

" The magistrates !" said Angus, trying to look bold, but trembling, and turning pale.

" The magistrates and the whole Bench of justices, who'll pretty soon let you know, and Mr. Ellerton know that you cannot break the law at your pleasure, or keep poor women locked up as if they were wild beasts—to say nothing of something I suspect about a gentleman who came here once upon a time, and has never been seen since."

Angus started—then gripping his fingers round the staff of his bill-hook, he looked at Jane as if not quite knowing what to do; whether to try and laugh it off, or show her the danger of speaking what she thought.

But Jane never flinched ; she took no notice of his gesture, but, assuming an innocent air, looked at him as if she had had no meaning in her words, yet at the same time showing that she was not to be frightened.

" As to your mother," said Angus, slowly un-clasping his hands, and making believe he had not heard what she had said, " it's not for me to say you shan't or shall go in. They're master's orders, not mine, and you know well enough the reason why he gave them, and what you did to make him turn against you."

" Oh, I know what you mean ; but bless you,

that's nothing. *I* am easily to be persuaded to hold my tongue (that is if I may see mother when I want)—not else. Besides, it would be the best thing you could do, for then I could put a stop to the talk in the town, and say that the house is *not* haunted, that there is *not* somebody shut up in it, and that mother and I can vouch for everything being as it should be; which at present I for one can't say, but have to undergo a great deal of trouble in consequence."

Angus paused at this, and appeared to be reflecting if it might not be as well to be a little less strict after what she said about the talk in the town, and the danger that might arise in suffering it to continue. The thought, too, that she might carry out her threat of going before the magistrates, and tell them what she suspected (and she evidently suspected something), decided him, and induced him to try and quiet her by saying—

" Suppose now I *was* to let you in; what then? How could you be better off, or your mother either? Couldn't you just as well now come here and let me tell you how she is, and if she has anything to say to you? I should think that would answer the same purpose, and save me getting into trouble if master caught me disobeying him."

"What! make you our go-between? No! if I ain't good enough to go into the house, I ain't good enough to meet you, and shan't trouble you again you may depend upon it. But as for your master ———"

"Well, what of him?"

"Let him just mind what he's about, that's all, or sure as I'm alive I'll do something dreadful to him, and make him shake in his shoes for treating me and mother as he does."

She was turning with the intention of leaving him, when Angus called to her, and begged her to remain, saying she should see her mother if she would only promise not to ask questions, or busy herself with what took place in the house.

"If," said he, "you have a mind to keep a quiet tongue, and not meddle or make with what does not concern you—why you may come and go as often as you please. That is, so long as master does not see you, and you'll swear your Bible oath not to say I told you you might go in, or mention in the town anything about what you see and hear."

"Not I, Angus. Bless you, I was not born yesterday! I knew Mr. Ellerton of old, and if the truth must be told, hate him too much to let his name soil my lips. If I am not to say any harm of him, you may take my word for it

I shan't say any good, and so your precious master and yourself may rest content you have nothing to fear from me."

"Mind you keep to that! Mind how you do as you have promised, and come and go without making mischief, or sure as my name's Angus you'll repent it. I have sworn to keep by master, to be true to master, and obey his orders. I have never been false to him as yet— except in letting you go in contrary to his orders. But don't you make bad use of it, or try to do him harm through that, else, spite of all your pretty looks, and the love you know as well as I do I can't hide from you, I'll do you a mischief, and curse you for the wickedest jade that ever lived!"

As he wished to give her the opportunity to slip into the house without his seeing her, he turned his back, and walked off in a direction where he thought he should make sure of meeting her on her return, and perhaps of talking to her, after what he had done to put her in good humour. Jane did not require a second hint, but as soon as he turned away she ran towards the house, and when far enough off not to be heard, favoured him with a parting word, and let him know exactly what she thought of him—but in the strictest confidence to herself.

"Infinitely obliged to you, I am sure," said Jane. "It's quite an unexpected pleasure to be obliged to you, and one I hope your master wont find out till the mischief's done, and then who cares if he knows it or not? I don't, and you may tell him so if you like. But I mean to do it for all that, and defy the pair of you to prevent it. Yes, mean to do it, do you hear, you louting, heavy-headed fellow? You stupid fellow! and you goose of a fellow! who think yourself so clever, yet can't see an inch before your nose? Much obliged to you for all that, and now you may go and hang yourself if you like, while I beg to remain your much obliged and very truly yours, Jane Botcherby."

Making a mocking curtsey, and bowing with an affected air towards him, she went inside the house, but shuddered at the desolate look of the passages and the deserted appearance of the rooms. The kitchen and the housekeeper's room were at the end of a long passage, and near the corridor which, at the best of times, Jane had a horror of, and now especially, for she could not help fancying that she saw her master hiding and stealing after her, and did not feel quite so confident as she wished.

But as it was of no use being afraid (not that she could help it) she put a bold face on it, and

walked towards her mother's room as if she had
been in the habit of going there, and had not
been threatened with all kinds of punishments if
caught in the house again. The housekeeper's
room was empty; so was the kitchen, and,
though she called, her mother did not answer,
and, what was worse, could not be found!

What was she to do? She had come on
purpose to see her (at least, she said so), and
now she had contrived to get into the house,
could not find her! They had not killed her,
she hoped, though she thought them wretches
enough for anything. That was not likely, for
her mother was of use to them, and would not
think of doing her master an injury even if she
could. Most probably she had gone out for a
little walk, or was busy somewhere close at
hand, or——

A slow and heavy tread coming along the corridor, and then a little husky cough, told her that
her mother was not only alive but stirring about
the place, and looking after her master's wants,
or obeying his orders in a manner that made her
blood run cold even to think about. But as it
would not do to say what she thought just then,
or let her know what she had discovered, she
crept along by the side of the wall, and saw her
mother coming from the direction of the old

porch-way, her form just visible in the ill-lighted passage, and that was all.

They were nearly face to face before Mrs. Botcherby saw her, and, on seeing her, she was so alarmed, that she dropped a tray she carried in her hands with the remains of food left on it, then screamed and screamed, and appeared so violently agitated, that Jane feared she would have fallen down in a fit, and had some difficulty in making her understand who she was, and that she was not some other woman of whom she might have reason to be afraid if she met her by herself.

" And couldn't you have gone somewhere else ?" cried Mrs. Botcherby, " or waited in the kitchen, and not come creeping about frightening one, and making me fancy it was somebody who had got away perhaps, and wanted to strangle me ?"

" Why, mother, how you talk !" said Jane. "There's no one but you and I in the whole house, unless it's some one else who is kept locked up, and not supposed to be anybody, now the mighty master has made up his mind to be a devil incarnate."

" Hold your tongue, hussy, and don't let me catch you talking in that way, or I'll be the death of you ! The devil, indeed ! The son of my old master is a gentleman, and people should make allowances for a little oddness in his temper."

"Allowances, indeed!" said Jane. "Well, how you can talk in that way is surprising! You, of all people, who must know how cruelly he uses his wife, and keeps her——"

"You have no prudence, no consideration——"

"No, I haven't, nor have other people either, for they begin to talk of what is going on here pretty freely, I can tell you. For my part I shouldn't wonder if all the old servants were to come in a body some night and break the place open, and not let him keep a poor lady shut up like a mad woman."

"Who said she was shut up? I didn't; and I should like to know what business people have to go talking of what they don't understand. A mad woman, indeed! She may be a little light-headed at times, and cause master a deal of trouble; but it does not follow that he neglects her, or treats her badly because of that."

"Not a bit of it, mother; and so I tell people when they say he does. But then it must be very dull and wretched for you to be shut up here, and kept in this hole of a place with no one to come near you, or say a word to you whether you are ill or well. Now, if I could only come and see you now and then, and look after you, I should, of course, be able to attend to you and take care of you; and then you know you wouldn't be quite so much under the thumb as you are of that good-for-nothing man of his, who had the impudence to make a fuss about my coming into the house, and even objected to my asking how you were."

"I shouldn't wonder. But then you see he's useful to master just now, and that I suppose makes him take upon himself more than he ought, and more than I'll let him if he don't mind what he's about."

"And doesn't that strike you as being odd, mother? Doesn't it appear strange that a gentleman of Mr. Ellerton's consequence should take up with a fellow like that, and be on familiar terms with him, while he is so grand and mighty with other people?"

"Sometimes. But I suppose he finds he can trust him and drive him about just as he likes."

"Or perhaps he's in his power, mother, and doesn't like to quarrel with him for fear he might turn round on him and tell people more about his doings than he would wish. Now, it has often struck me——"

Further talk was put a stop to by the sudden slamming of a door, and then a heavy footstep ascending the stairs, which the stillness enabled

them to detect as being that of Mr. Ellerton,
returned from his walk, and no doubt requiring
to be waited on immediately.

There was no time to be lost. The old housekeeper began bustling about and Jane helping
her, until his meal was ready, when she made
an excuse to go away lest he should see her and
storm the place down at finding her in the house.
Angus she knew was waiting for her, and as she,
did not wish to have anything to say to him, she
kissed her mother, said she would come and see
her again soon, and the moment the old woman
had gone up with the dinner, she ran down the
corridor, and so out by the old porch leading to
the evergreens.

Mr. Ellerton and her mother were safe for the
present, and Angus would not stir, as she well
knew, but would wait in hopes of meeting her as
she went back. A better opportunity she could
not have, but now she had got it, she hardly
dared to move for fear of being seen or heard
stirring about closer than might be thought safe
or prudent.

Yes, there was the outside room; the door
chained up and the grated window high above
her reach. Could she climb up there and look
inside, she might see and speak with her mistress,
discover her wretched state, and say a word of

comfort to her, if she could only understand her, and not fly into a fit of raving at hearing herself addressed in a voice she knew.

But as she looked, and longed to have the power to get up to the window, she saw a pair of thin, white hands clasp round the iron bars, grasping and clinging to them, and tearing at them, in the vain hope to wrench them away.

The sight of those thin hands, the frantic grasps, and the useless efforts to force away the bars, struck her as something terrible; and though she longed to try her strength as well, and help her mistress in her insane effort to escape, she knew its uselessness, and that if her liberty depended upon that, she must remain a prisoner for the remainder of her life, unless she could be rescued by other means.

Feebler and feebler grew the efforts, the action less, until the fighting of those thin, white hands quieted at last, when they unloosed their hold, and a heavy fall was heard, as if her mistress had slipped, and fallen from the window to which she had evidently found means to climb.

She heard her scream, and then her feeble moans, while a low, sad sobbing came from that prison-like room in which her brutal husband kept her, to punish her for no fault of hers, and gratify his hatred and revenge on a poor, miserable, demented woman.

She could not bear it. She could not endure the thought of what she suffered, and had half a mind to run off to the town for assistance. But she could not. She did not dare to inform people of what she had seen, for fear her husband should be tempted to carry her away, and interfere with the arrangements they had made for punishing him effectually.

There would come a time, but till it came, Jane had the greatest difficulty in restraining herself, and not screaming or calling to her mistress to let her know (not that she thought she would understand her) that there was help at hand, and coming from a quarter she little expected, if she would only endure a little longer, and comfort herself with the reflection that her troubles would soon be over.

Stay there she could not. She felt she should go mad herself if she stood any longer listening to those fretful cries. Her mistress might scream again!—beat herself against the walls, or climb up to the window and fall again! She could not endure that. She knew she should do something desperate, and at the very moment that she heard her beating at the door and calling out for help again, she took to her heels and ran!—kept under

the shelter of the trees till she was clear of the
house, then ran again, and never slackened in
her speed until she found herself in the open
road on the outskirts of the town, and far away
from the spot where Angus was expecting
her.

CHAPTER IV.

THE permission once given, Jane did not wait
for a second, but went to see her mother whenever she had a mind.   She had plenty of excuses.
Her mother's health was uncertain ; and, like a
dutiful daughter, Jane paid her daily visits, sat
with her, or helped her in her work, and soon
became so necessary to her that Mrs. Botcherby
would not have parted with her, or stayed in the
place without the privilege of seeing her, on any
consideration.

She never saw Mr. Ellerton, although from
certain hints her mother dropped, she was certain
he knew of her going to the house, but did not
dare to forbid her for fear of her talking and
setting other people to talk as well.

Be that as it might, no one ever said a word
to her on the subject, for her mother carefully
avoided all mention of the doings of the house;
while Angus made a point of meeting her whenever she came or went, as Jane sometimes thought,
as if set to watch her and keep an eye upon her
movements.

But one night, just as Jane was leaving, her mother was taken so ill with a fit of her old complaint, it was arranged that she should stay and sit up with her, she not being well enough to be left alone. Luckily for the old woman she got better after a night's rest; but the mischief was done. Jane had been permitted to remain one night in the house, and it would be her own fault if she did not improve the occasion and stop as many as she liked.

She had no chance of finding out anything. Her mother forbade her talking, and spoke so sharply if she at any time inquired after her mistress, that she gave over the attempt, and made up her mind to watch, but say nothing. The same routine was gone through every day. The meals were got ready; and regularly at a certain hour she saw her mother place a supply of food upon a tray and take it down the corridor, open the porch door, and go towards the outside room. But as Angus was always there to meet her, and as Jane did not wish to let them see that she was observing them, she held her tongue, but felt convinced that Angus was ordered to stand at the door from the time the old woman carried in the tray until she came out, in order to prevent her going in.

The food had nearly always disappeared when

the tray was brought back, though sometimes it remained untouched, or lay scattered about as if it had been refused or cast aside in anger. But as she had resolved to say nothing she took no notice, though every time her mother left, she crept after her, saw the same thing repeated every day, and not unfrequently heard distressing cries come from the outside room as soon as her mother left, and Angus had chained and fastened up the door.

What was she to do. No visitors were admitted to the house, and no intercourse was kept up with any one, for Angus warned off strangers, and brought their supply of food himself from the town, so that there was no necessity for any one to call, and no likelihood of people interfering with what they chose to do, provided they kept their own counsel and Jane could be prevailed upon to remain quiet where she was.

The appearance of strangers about the place was so unusual, that Ellerton was not a little surprised when he saw two gentlemen come down the carriage-drive, a few days after Jane had been there, walking towards the house, and talking together in earnest conversation. One of them was dressed in black, and had a staid and serious air, while the other flourished a small cane, or, making passes in the air, whipped off the top of a flower-stalk with the precision of a fencing master.

Who could they be?   He knew nothing of them, and, annoyed at their intrusion, he called to Angus to turn them back and warn them off the premises.   But as he looked and watched again, he fancied that he had seen the shorter of the two before; the little, bolt-upright and consequential man, strutting and flourishing his cane, · and making the most out of a little.

Of course he had.   It was the undersized Captain he had met at Mr. Blissett's, and had longed to thrash for his impertinence.   But the other, who was he?   That tall, well-figured man?   He had the appearance of a clergyman, and kept looking up at the house as he came along, and pointing it out to his companion.

But Angus had gone to them, that was one comfort, and would soon get rid of them.   No! They were evidently in altercation, and did not seem disposed to turn back so quietly as he expected.   Angus appeared obstinate and determined; but the others seemed determined too, and by their manner led him to suppose that they had resolved on seeing him; for, though the clergyman expostulated, the little man looked terribly indignant, and whipped his cane as if threatening to lay it across his servant's shoulders.

Why did not Angus snatch it from him, and break it across his back? He wished he had, and almost expected he would, but for the clergyman's intercession, who made a show of peacemaking, and of endeavouring to pacify the Captain, by which means Ellerton had a good opportunity of looking at him and of observing him attentively. His face was towards the window now, and as he gazed at him he thought he detected a likeness to some one he had seen before, that struck him with amazement.

Despite the horror and the dread with which that face inspired him, he kept his eyes fixed on it; stared at it, and endeavoured to recall the features of the miniature! Tried to match them with it, and satisfy himself it was not the same, though so nearly alike it appeared next to impossible that any one person could so closely resemble another and yet be different. For he *was* different. His dress was different, so were his manners and his bearing. He had no moustache, and did not seem quite so tall; but, for all that, the likeness was so strong he could hardly convince himself that he was deceived, until he looked again, when he felt certain it was not the same, though the resemblance was so strong he might have been easily pardoned for making a mistake.

He had barely time to recover himself before Angus came to say that it was of no use telling them they couldn't come ; they said they would, and insisted on seeing his master in spite of him.

" And what—what do they want with me ?"

" They did not say, master ; but gave me these cards, and said you would know who they were."

On one was engraved the name of the Rev. Mr. Arkwright ; on the other, Lieutenant Conroy Nubbleton.

" Arkwright," said Ellerton, " I don't remember the name. The other I do remember, but what business he can have with me I cannot imagine."

He was about repeating his orders for Angus to deny him, and. refuse them admittance, when he heard the Captain's heels clinking up the stairs, and the other following him.

They had reached the room, and were walking in, when Ellerton, springing to his feet, stept forward, and haughtily demanded to know the reason of their unauthorized intrusion into his house after his servant had informed them that they were not to be admitted.

" Mr. Ellerton," said the Captain, bowing stiffly, and advancing into tho room with the utmost stateliness. " You will, I am sure, excuse our want of courtesy in walking so rudely into your house ; but there are times and seasons when the usual good manners which should at all times distinguish gentlemen must be forgotten for the sake of important and imperative duty."

" Be good enough to explain it, then. I have no time to waste, and shall thank you to be brief."

" In the first place, then," said the Captain, quite as grandly as Ellerton, and not in the least put out, " I must beg the honour to introduce my friend, the Reverend Mr. Arkwright. Mr. Arkwright, Mr. Ellerton."

" Well, sir, and what then ?" said Ellerton in reply. " As I do not know the gentleman, and never heard his name before, I cannot very well understand what business he can have with me, or why people who call themselves gentlemen should so far forget the courtesies of society as to intrude where they have no right, and demand to see me whether I will or no."

" That, sir," replied the Captain, rather more grandly than before, " depends on circumstances, and may be excused when a gentleman so far forgets those usages of society as to empower a rude, unpolished menial to refuse admittance to gentlemen who express a wish to see him, without first satisfying himself what they want, and assuring himself that he is dealing with gentlemen who would not submit to be insulted with impunity."

"Oh, indeed," said Ellerton, glancing from the Captain to the reverend gentleman as if he felt that *he* were the important person in the interview, and that to him he must look for an explanation of their strange behaviour.

" Yes, sir, and *indeed*," the Captain answered, emphasizing the latter word, and drawing himself up in front of Ellerton as if to convince him that he was quite ready to meet him, and exchange shots behind a haystack at a moment's notice.

But Ellerton was cold and calm. He had recovered his first surprise, and was not so easily excited as the Captain. He had had time to reflect that some matter of importance was likely to be discussed, and, fixing his eye uneasily on the reverend gentleman, he passed over the other as if he were of no consequence.

"Permit me to explain," said the reverend gentleman, speaking for the first time. " Our visit is not one of pleasure, but necessity, and has reference to a subject of the highest importance, not only as it affects us personally, but as it concerns you, and therefore I should wish we might discuss it calmly, but seriously, and give our best attention to the investigation of a very distressing occurrence we have too much reason to fear has recently taken place either in or near your house."

There was nothing in his manner to indicate what he meant, nor were his words explanatory of anything that bore on Ellerton especially. Yet he looked as if they did—endeavoured to appear calm, but could not, and though he kept his eyes still fixed, he felt his cheek grow pale, and his brow moisten with a visible perspiration as he met the reverend gentleman face to face, and stood as if expecting him to proceed.

But as he did not, and as the pause became more awkward the longer it lasted, he knit his brows, and prepared to question in his turn.

"By all means. Gentlemen of your cloth prefer to be serious, and, since you wish it, I see no objection to what you propose, if you will only come to this wonderful something, and have done with it. The subject rests with you, not with me, and since it is no doubt highly interesting, I am prepared to listen; though what on earth I have to do with the matter exceeds my comprehension."

"Pardon me. The subject to which I would allude not only refers to you directly, but points

to the people of your house so unmistakably, that I
shall be glad to receive such an explanation of
your own and their conduct as shall set my
doubts at rest, and relieve my mind of the suspicions I entertain respecting the recent disappearance of my beloved brother. It is my painful
duty to have to inquire into this, and though I
have every desire to treat you with respect, I must
tell you plainly that I shall expect the fullest
assistance at your hands to enable us to institute
a searching inquiry into what has become of him,
and here in your house, where, as we have some
reason to believe, we may hear something respecting him."

"Here !" said Ellerton, nerving himself for
what was to come next, and fully prepared to
meet it with indifference. "I am entirely at a
loss to understand what you mean by 'here ;'
but as you have, no doubt, good reasons for
what you do, I shall be glad to assist you as far
as I can, though in what way it is impossible for
me to know. Will you be seated ?"

Having waited till they took their seats, he
sat with his back towards the light, and coolly
asked—

"And may I request to be informed who was
your brother ? Your name, I perceive, is Arkwright—the Reverend Mr. Arkwright. Your

brother's, I presume, was Arkwright too? I regret exceedingly not having heard of him or you before. I am fortunate in recognising the name upon the other card, 'Lieutenant Conroy Nubbleton.' Yes, I am fortunate there. I do remember having heard that name, and am happy to be reminded of it before it escaped my memory."

The Captain would not have borne this insult patiently, but his friend was about to speak, and though he looked with the greatest possible contempt at Ellerton, and rapped his boots with his cane in sign of what he would wish to do with it, he held his tongue, but had to clench his teeth to keep it within bounds.

" My brother was, as you say, of the same name as myself. His name was Frederick Arkwright, and I shall be glad to know if you at any time heard that name before?"

" Never."

" And did you never see him?"

This question rather startled Ellerton, but by fencing with it he hoped to avoid the difficulty, and gain time.

" I may; I cannot answer. It is quite impossible for me to say whether I may have seen a person I do not know."

" That is not what I mean. I mean, have you

by any chance met him, and, if so, upon what terms? Here in your house, or in the neighbouring town ?"

" I have already stated," said Ellerton, placing his hand in his pocket to be certain that the miniature was safe, and where he always kept it, " my entire ignorance of your brother's name, which I now hear for the first time, or of himself personally, which I regret, as I have no doubt he bore a family likeness to yourself."

" As far as our personality is concerned we are, or were, alike ; but our habits were different. I therefore ask you again (allowing you to judge of him by me) whether you ever met him, or knew of him either by that name or any other ?"

" I really must protect myself against this cross-examination, and beg to state emphatically that I am at a loss to understand the meaning of your and your friend's intrusion, or of your inquiries on a subject totally indifferent to me. It would be strange, indeed, if I were to be held responsible for runaway schoolboys, or truant sons, or brothers, as the case may be."

" You will be good enough to understand that my brother was no schoolboy. He was a man quite as capable of independent action as yourself, and quite as capable of resenting. insult as any man alive."

The sudden energy that accompanied these words, the flush, the kindling eye, the entire change in his whole demeanour, and the indignant glance he cast on Ellerton, struck him with amazement, and drew his attention to him in too marked a manner not to be observed.

The change was only momentary. Before Ellerton had time to do more than wonder at the alteration in his face, or stare at him in astonishment, the other had resumed his former staid expression, and became as suddenly transformed to his old self as if that flush had never mounted to his cheek, and the indignant glance never come to light his eye.

"It may be necessary," resumed the reverend gentleman, after a moment's pause, "that I should acquaint you who my brother was, and how positioned. He was in the army, and about to join his regiment in India, when an unlooked-for illness prevented his leaving England so soon as he intended, with the lady to whom he was engaged, and hoped to marry."

"He recovered at last, I hope."

"He did, but not to meet the happiness he expected, since the lady to whom he was engaged had been induced to believe that he had neglected her, and, persuaded by her mother, bestowed her hand upon another better suited to her selfish notions of personal advantage."

. "He proved himself deserving of the honour, I have no doubt."

"I cannot answer that so confidently as I could wish. Let us hope he did, and that my brother's loss was more than compensated by the affection and attention he bestowed on her. Be that as it may, she was, as I have stated, engaged to him and married before my brother could recover strength to prevent their union, or explain the reason of his presumed neglect."

"I sympathise with him sincerely, and wish with all my heart that it had happened differently."

"He was, as I am informed, distracted at her loss, and would instantly have gone abroad had not an unexpected accident altered his views, and kept him in London contrary to his original intention."

"Indeed. May I venture to inquire what it was?"

"Certainly. He lost an uncle during his stay in London, and at his death became possessed of his entire fortune. He was now rich—rich and independent of the world, and resigning his appointment, he resolved to stay where he was, and give up all thoughts of leaving England."

"I can fully enter into your feelings. Pray

proceed. The story becomes interesting now the poor young man has grown so suddenly rich."

" The settlement of his affairs compelled him to remain in town longer than he expected; but as soon as they could be arranged, he suddenly disappeared—quitted London—and from that time to this has left no clue by which he could be traced, earnestly as his friends and family desired to know what had become of him."

" Indeed! How comes it, then, that he was traced down here? That is, how came you to imagine that he might be discovered in this neighbourhood?"

" Weeks passed by," the reverend gentleman continued, without noticing the interruption, " before he wrote, and even then he preserved a strict silence as to the motive of his absence; simply communicated the fact that he was well, but left his family in the same state of grief at his extraordinary behaviour. I will not pay so bad a compliment to your penetration as to assure you that it was not to the contents of that letter we were indebted for our intelligence, or were led to suppose that he might be found ' down here' by what he wrote at that particular time."

" You saw that by the postmark, I suppose," said Ellerton, feeling the necessity of saying something, though he would rather have kept silent.

"That might, indeed, have furnished a clue, were additional evidence wanted, to show that on the very day he wrote home to his mother (as can be proved) he was seen at the inn in the neighbouring town where he had been staying from the time he quitted London, but which he left on that very night, and has never been heard of since."

"There is nothing very singular in that," said Ellerton, endeavouring to treat the matter lightly, though he felt the net draw closer round him at every word.

"My mother wrote to him in reply; begged and entreated him to write to her again immediately, and relieve her of the anxiety she felt on his account. He did not write. So she wrote again; but not receiving an answer, wrote and wrote again, until she became so seriously alarmed at his continued silence, my father sent for me; begged of me to take his place, as he was too ill to travel, and use every effort in my power to find out what had become of him."

"You found him at last, I hope," said Ellerton, growing more and more uneasy.

"It was my good fortune to be able to obtain a clue to him by an accidental meeting with the gentleman who had the management of his affairs on my road to London, from whom I obtained direct information as to the state of his feelings during the time he was acting for him, and previously to his quitting town; of his ceaseless grief, and of his constantly-expressed determination to see the lady of whom he felt he had been robbed, and convince her of his constancy, though she had failed in hers.

" Did he succeed ?" said Ellerton, betraying by his manner an earnestness little in keeping with his former coldness.

" That is not so sure ; though it is tolerably certain that he saw the lady during her stay in town, at a theatre or a concert, and maddened by her sight, appeared more bent than ever (so his lawyer said) on seeing her again."

" Oh! at a theatre was it ?" said Ellerton, with sudden earnestness.

" Or some such place, where it might naturally be expected she would go, and where my brother, doubtless, hoped to see her."

" And did her husband know of this, or was he so blinded by his love that he suspected nothing, and did not detect the signs of recognition passing between them ?"

" I cannot tell. I do not know ; but by his hurrying her away, and keeping her secluded from society, it may fairly be presumed that he saw something which excited his fears, and determined him to remove her where she would be placed entirely under his control. It is also to be presumed that my brother was sensible of this, for he shortly after quitted London, as it is presumed, with the intention of concealing himself somewhere about the neighbourhood in hopes he might see her, or communicate with her in secret."

" And did he—did he accomplish this—or did her husband fathom his design, and discover it in time to prevent him ?"

" Of that nothing is known. One thing, however, *is* known, and it has now become a matter of the gravest importance—that on one particular night her husband was observed to look at him in a strange, suspicious manner, in the High Street of the town, and watch him from the other side of the way. It is also known, that on the very night my brother can be proved to have gone near his house in company with a girl belonging to his household—he —the husband, was seen riding towards it, dashing along at a desperate speed, and evidently hastening home on some important errand."

Close and closer drew the net! That girl! that very girl who had been the chief cause of his misery, was now to be brought against him to prove him guilty of complicity in that brother's death. His very ride from London tracked and explained, from point to point, until the end was reached—and the missing man traced up to him.

"The facts are as I have stated," said Mr. Arkwright. "It remains for you to explain them away, or give a different meaning to them than what they assume at present. My brother has not been seen since the time he set his foot within your doors, and as nothing has been heard of him either by the person who led him there, nor by the people in the town—I ask you, Mr. Ellerton, if *you* know what has become of him; whether you are cognizant of his death, or whether some one in your house has had a hand in dispatching him? It must be one or the other; and I expect not only the fullest explanation at your hands, but a clear and precise account of what you know respecting him."

At every word—at every fresh accumulated evidence, Ellerton betrayed increased anxiety. His lips opened, but he did not speak; his eyes were steadfast, yet they did not see; and slowly thinking what to say or do, he let some little time pass by before he ventured to reply.

"And do you think," he said at last, "that

because your brother was a fool, and suffered himself to be coaxed over to meet some girl he had picked up—and who, for aught I know, may have been a member of my household—that therefore I am responsible for his folly, through his disreputable association with the girl? That is too monstrous and absurd to be entertained even for a moment; and I am surprised, gentlemen, and not only surprised but indignant, that you could be induced by a ridiculous notion of this sort to cast suspicion upon me, or make me accountable for his low amours. The most likely thing that I can suppose is, that he has gone off with the girl somewhere, and not wishing to have his connexion with her made public, keeps himself carefully concealed."

" But would he leave his luggage at the inn? go off without taking that with him, and leave his mother's letters unopened on the table? Would he do that? Would he, presuming he is alive— which I doubt—would he neglect his duty so far as to expose her to the misery his silence would be sure to entail on her?"

" He might. I cannot say. Men have left all things before now to please a foolish—sometimes a wilful fancy."

" Doubtless. But then the girl is left behind as well. Does not that seem strange. He would have no object in leaving her, but, according to your showing—would have taken her away at least. But she is here. Here, in this very house, for we saw her as we came along, and had no difficulty in recognising her by the description we had given of her. Should you, however, doubt the truth of what we say—pray call her up and let her answer for herself."

"This is beyond endurance! What, call up my servants; inquire of them, and interrogate them about their master's conduct? No. If you must question, question somewhere else, but not here. This is my house, and I will not permit myself to be insulted any longer in it, either by you or anybody else."

By affecting a show of violence, and speaking in a lofty style, Ellerton thought to alarm, or at the least to make them careful how they ventured to excite his anger. But he was mistaken. Instead of making them draw back, or apologise, he found to his surprise that the reverend gentleman assumed an air of positive defiance— while the Captain swelled and bristled up, slapped his little padded chest, and, indignant at the thought of what he, as a soldier and a gentleman, had been forced to put up with in the cause of peace—was on the point of giving force to some terrific menace, when the reverend gentlemen stepped between and spoke as follows :—

"Mr. Ellerton. Having been informed of my brother's visit to your house, and of his subsequent disappearance, I was in hopes you would have been the first to lend your help to take off suspicion from yourself, and next from those who are in your service. But as you have shown a disinclination to accept this favour at our hands, and set yourself in opposition to us— I beg distinctly to inform you that I shall endeavour by every justifiable means to sift this mystery to the bottom. I shall make it a point of duty to carry out my search by diligent inquiry, and I give you full notice, that willingly as I would have received your excuses at the first, and accepted them if I found them reasonable—I shall utterly distrust and doubt you now. I shall look upon you, if not as the actual perpetrator, yet as an aider and abettor in my brother's death, and by every agency that the law can put in force, shall endeavour to bring it home to you. Good morning, sir."

But the Captain had something to say. The moment his friend had left the room, he turned to Ellerton, and favoured him with a few parting words on his own account.

"It has not escaped my observation that you used the word 'ridiculous' in reference to myself and my friend ; you likewise repeated the word ' intrusion,' and led us to believe that you meant to apply those terms to us. I have given you ample time to apologise by the pause I have just made ; but since you do not seem disposed to avail yourself of the opportunity, nor to retract the offensive appellations, I beg emphatically to tell you that you are no gentleman. You are a bully and a coward ; and though I cannot pretend to compete with you in bodily strength, you shall find that, as a soldier and a gentleman, I am able to protect myself by the weapons usually employed on such occasions, and as I am the person demanding satisfaction, shall leave the choice of them to you. I am to be heard of at the Green Dragon, and shall be happy to be favoured with the name of your friend. Mr. Ellerton, I have the honour to wish you good morning."

Throwing the door wide open, to enable him to make his exit with becoming dignity, Captain Conroy Nubbleton made a formal bow, put his cane under his arm, turned on his heel, and meeting the reverend gentleman outside, he put his arm in his, and took him, as it were, under his protection, carefully withheld from him the knowledge that he had challenged Ellerton, and sincerely hoping that he might accept it, walked away in company with him.

CHAPTER V.

DOUBTS.

No sooner were they gone than the full force of the danger of his position became apparent. He had tried to laugh and turn it off, as something beneath his notice; but now he was alone, and had time to think, he saw the precipice on which he stood, and knew that the slightest indiscretion or wavering on his part would send him over, and utterly complete his ruin.

What was he to do? He knew enough to be satisfied that he was in danger, but not the full extent of his jeopardy. He could not tell how far they had traced his connexion with the supposed death of young Arkwright, and was therefore powerless to defend himself. That his interrogators had not stated the whole of what they knew was easily perceived, and it was also easy to see that they purposely kept back the chief part of the charge with a view to prevent his preparing himself beforehand, and defending himself from his presumed guilt, until the time had come when they could bring it home, and make him answer for his offences to the law.

It was impossible for him to ascertain how far they had proceeded in their search, or if they had been assisted in it by some one who knew more of his proceedings than he was aware. He could answer for himself, but not for others. He knew of nothing he had done that could be brought in actual evidence against him; and as to the law, if those who were chiefly interested in remaining silent kept their own counsel, there was little fear of discovery, still less of his being made a party to the crime.

He was not so foolish as to question the power of the law, or set himself in opposition to it. He knew its power, and he dreaded it; dreaded it the more, perhaps, because he felt that he was guilty, and that, safe as he thought himself, some unexpected omission, or some incautious word, might be brought against him, to show that he knew more about it than he was willing to admit, and that young Arkwright's death might fairly be brought home to him, little as he saw the possibility of such a chance at present, and willing, as he professed himself, to court inquiry, instead of flying from it.

But then how were they to find it out? how detect the fatal blow, or the hand that dealt it? His was the chief offence who killed. But then the law might punish the instigator with equal

7—2

severity as the actual perpetrator. It was not so easy to be blind to that. Indeed, he knew he could not, and therefore felt the increased danger of his position now it was discovered that he had been seen hastening home at the very time the crime had been committed, and might fairly be charged with some guilty knowledge, if not with the actual commission of the deed.

There was danger both ways. Danger in being suspected. Danger in being even spoken of in connexion with the young man's disappearance, and ceaseless apprehension now he knew the cry was up, and that those interested in his loss were on the alert to discover his murderer.

Let them! He would defy them still, and dare them to breathe a syllable against him. He was no coward to start at shadows. He was a man of fortune and position. A man whose reputation was unsullied, and whose name, question it as they might, would stand investigation with the best and noblest in the land. Why, then, should he fear, or entertain the doubt he did, or try to argue against the possibility of their connecting him, however remotely, with the alleged offence? Or had he a secret cause of fear; some dread that held him back, that made him less confident the more he thought about it?

He had! He knew it, though he would

scarcely admit it to himself. For that safeguard once cut through, he was as clearly liable to be indicted and tried for his life as the meanest cutthroat that ever took up murder as a trade, and dealt with human life as freely as he would barter a carcase, or traffic in the shambles.

That fear was Angus! True, he had trusted him; but he doubted him for all that, and above all, knew he was in his power. Should he but say a word, or hope to save his miserable life by sacrificing him, where then was he, and what became of his confidence, his superiority of position, and the fair name he boasted, if he but opened his mouth and spoke of what he knew?

There was no escape from that; no getting away from that degrading fear, that miserable, wretched doubt, that stepped between his pride and consequence, and made him feel he was the mere creature of another's will—the mouse in the cat's claws, the rat in the dog's mouth! Ignominy and contempt, rage and fear, all fighting in his breast, and making him feel more completely like a slave than even Angus had been to him; more cowed, and compelled to be submissive, if he but held his finger up, than a thief in a prison, or a felon in a dock.

Looked upon as a tool, and acting as a tool,

he had been accustomed to do with him as he chose, and treat him like a bondslave. But he now began to feel that he might have the power to hurt as well, and prove as dangerous to him as he had proved to others. It was only natural, perhaps, he should do so. He had had no motive in the act, no malice and no spite. He was the blind instrument of another's will, and feeling what he had done likely to recoil on himself, who knew how soon he might turn round on him, and make him pay the penalty of having trusted him?

Oh, how he longed to look into that man's mind, to read his thoughts, and be acquainted with the workings of his brain. He had saved his life, it was true; but what of that? Would he not try to save himself now he had the opportunity, and, like a drowning man, pull down another in his struggle to escape? He knew the value he attached to life—the store he set by it; and was it not reasonable to suppose he would resort to anything rather than lose it? Of course he would. He had no fine touch of honour; no constancy of a noble nature to make him superior to suffering, or to think of sacrificing himself to save his friend. He had but his brute instincts for his guide—his slavish, brutish instincts—and was it likely he would question what to do, or delay choosing between his own life and another's, if he had the chance of choosing?

He would! It was no use fighting against the nature of the man. He would be true to himself: try to make himself secure, and on the first approach of danger, expose his artifice, and betray him to the world.

If so, if his life had to be set against his own, would it not be as well to be beforehand with him, and deprive him of the power to do him injury by getting rid of him? Self-preservation was the universal rule; why should he scruple then to do what others did, or as Angus himself would do to make his own course clear. It was not a pleasant reflection. But it was forced on him by circumstances, and Ellerton, though he might shrink from the necessity, yielded, and prepared to act upon it.

"And is this to be the end?" he hurriedly exclaimed. "Shall one pernicious influence govern all, and change what I had hoped to be a blessing into a curse? Shall he who was the cause of this, sleep peacefully in his grave, and leave the living to endure the consequences of his wrong? be tortured with self-reproach, and inwardly repine, because of the punishment inflicted upon him, and wish perhaps, that he were living still? The fault was his, not mine. The

wife I lost was mine, and now when all is gone,
when happiness and hope are lost as well, remorse, and doubt, and fear are all that's left to
recompense the past."

"Was it not enough." he said, "to be deceived
and cheated, and left to find the grossness of the
imposition practised on me, but I must endure
the penalty of their evil doings, and be made
responsible for what followed ! Was it right
that I should be the scapegoat, the dupe of an
artful mother, and the cover of her daughter's
shame ? Was not all this enough, but that she
should still keep practising the deceit, carry it
on from day to day, and wilfully impose upon
me, until her lover could redeem his pawn, or
pass it off upon my hands again as though it
had been faultless !"

"What would they say of me," he cried,
"who in my early life endeavoured to persuade
me, that woman was not so perfect a creature as
I maintained her to be. Would they not turn
round on me, and laugh at me, and instance my
own wife as the best proof of their argument,
and the absurdity of mine ?—show me the weakness and the folly of my notions, and utterly
confound me by placing her conduct in powerful
contrast to the views I endeavoured to maintain,
and leave me the laughing-stock of those who

differed with me? But it is over now. The wife I chose as realizing my dream of bliss, and representing in herself the best and purest attribute of her sex—has cruelly and wilfully deceived me! She has heartlessly exposed me to disgrace, and therefore let her suffer the full extent of her worthlessness and sin."

Roused from his despondency by reflecting on his imagined wrongs, and determined, if possible, to secure himself against the consequences of the revenge he had taken, he instantly resolved to go in search of Angus; satisfy himself he could depend entirely on him, or take the readiest means to rid himself of the only witness, as he supposed, of the crime committed at his instigation, and by his order.

In case it should be found necessary to despatch him, he armed himself, and priming and loading a pistol, placed it in his coat-pocket, then quitting the room, drew the door softly after him, and, determined on what he had to do, went out to look for Angus, expecting to find him somewhere about the grounds, or sleeping in his old quarters in the Avenue.

"If," said he, "I find him true, and likely to stand by me to the last, I will endeavour to deserve his faith. I will prove my gratitude by placing him above the fear of want; hold by him like a friend, and never question his integrity in anything he does—if he only acts as I desire. But should I find him in the least deceitful, or uncertain, I will kill him, and kill him as secretly as he despatched the other."

CHAPTER VI.

SOMETHING HANDY.

ANGUS was nowhere to be seen in the grounds; so he went toward the Avenue, and after looking cautiously about, without perceiving him, he felt confident that he should be able to carry out his intention, and get rid of him without being suspected. That is, if it were necessary to get rid of him, and nothing remained but choosing between his own life and another's.

He could see the old porchway and the outside room, where he stood; the evergreens and the rearward of the house. But those he did not care to look at, for one and all reminded him of his brother and his wife. His brother long since dead and passed away, and his wife a prisoner in the very cage from which he had effected his escape.

Was he thinking of him? Picturing to his mind that dull and wretched room, the grated window, and the chained up door? His wife, too—was she present in his mind, and her miserable condition made a subject of thought? her fruitless efforts to free herself taken into consideration, and her unhappy state reflected on—or passed over with a pang, and then forgotten? Was his determination to carry out his barbarous intention as strong as ever, his resolve as firm, and his indignation towards her to be pursued with the same relentlessness as before? Were her cries to be unheeded, her shrieks unnoticed, and her sufferings to be looked upon as a just punishment for her offence in venturing to deceive him? Were these to be passed over; her day and night imprisonment to be regarded coldly and heartlessly; and her loss of reason to be attributed to her own fault, and not to his cruelty? Had he loved her, professed unbounded faith, then changed as suddenly, and, acting on supposition, condemned the woman he had loved to such a doom on mere suspicion?

It would not bear reflection, and despite his determination to carry out his own peculiar notions of revenge on his unoffending wife, the emotion he felt unnerved him for awhile, and made him doubtful of the justice of his conduct. But this soon passed. He had resolved, and the small whisperings of conscience failed to excite remorse, or to call up forgiveness for his imagined wrongs He had yet to seek out Angus, to see him, and talk with him, and then, perhaps, commit another crime; pile up the weight of his offences, and add another murder on his soul.

He turned away; then entering the Avenue, glanced towards the centre, where he saw Angus sitting on a log of a tree, either asleep or deep in thought. He never moved, never heard him as he came tramping through the fallen leaves; but sitting on the log, clasped the staff of the billhook with his hands, and leaned his head on them.

He was close upon him before his servant observed him, and was beginning to wonder what he could be doing, when Angus heard his steps, and starting to his feet, swung round his billhook, then let it fall when he saw his master, and said he thought it was some one else.

Ellerton looked at him, but said nothing. He saw he was alarmed, and trembled, though at what he could not tell. His eyes were wild, his face was haggard, and his whole deportment so altered, he knew there must be some cause for his emotion, and then began to think that probably the fear of being discovered had changed him from the stalwart, if uncouth, being he had formerly been, into the shaking culprit he now beheld, trembling and aghast, and afraid of his own shadow.

But the change was not singular in Angus.

His master had changed as well, and bore the trace of recent suffering so plainly stamped upon him, that even Angus, little as he might be supposed to be a quick observer, saw the change, and marked it as he stood looking at him, and respectfully awaiting what he had to say.

Was it, as Angus thought, that his master was as much tormented as himself; as sleepless, and as much a prey to fear? Or was he different in his nature, and less susceptible to the horrid sights and noises that followed him wherever he went, and made his life a misery? He did not envy him either way ; for if *he* was frightened at a rustling in the trees, his master might suffer as much or more from other causes, though he had a different way of showing it.

It was of no use for either of them to affect indifference. They were the same, although different, and, connected by a mutual guilt, experienced a mutual fear. They were evidently afraid of one another; and eyeing about them distrustfully, appeared to be on the watch lest the one should take advantage of the other; while Ellerton, conscious of his own design, secretly suspected a similar intention in Angus, yet made it appear that he confided in him, and trusted him, and would have placed his life in his hands.

" Angus," he said at last, and after the pause

had lasted longer than seemed necessary, " I
have come to speak with you. Sit down—not
there, but close by my side, so that I may
whisper what I have to say and have no fear
of being overheard, in case any one should be
hiding among the trees."

Angus did as he was ordered, and sitting on
the old log of a tree drawn crossways over the
hollow in the ground, patiently waited what his
master had to say.

" It is no news to tell you," Ellerton began,
still true to his old selfishness, and confirmed of
his superior hold upon his man, " nor do I wish
to remind you of the obligation under which I
have placed you, and the life of gratitude I
might demand of you had I the desire to exact
it. But I do not. I simply want you to be
true to me, and prove your willingness to assist
me in anything I may require at your hands."

" It's not like Angus, master, to say one thing
and mean another; and I don't think you have
reason to find fault with me in that respect, and
have besides no cause to fear I would not obey
your orders, if I can only see my way to what
you want."

" There is no fear—no present fear at least;
and I am not going to ask you to do anything
fresh, but simply to be silent on what has passed."

"That's easy enough, master. I know how
to keep a quiet tongue between my teeth, and
ain't so fond of talking of what's not over safe
to talk about at all.   It's not my talking,
master, you need be afraid of.   It's the talk of
other people and of the justices which makes
me uncomfortable at times, lest they should find
out what took place up at the house yonder a
little while ago."

"The justices!   And what have the justices,
as you call them, to do with me, or why should
you imagine that they could associate my name
with what you did?" said Ellerton, wishing to
be informed how far his man was willing to take
the responsibility on himself, and relieve him
from any blame in what had happened.   "You
could not surely be so ungrateful as to betray
me, or involve me in any danger you might
run, were you suspected and arrested on the
charge?"

"I don't know, master.   It's difficult to say
till the time comes what a man might do to save
his life.   But I suppose——"

"Suppose nothing, but tell me this: were the
officers ready to arrest you, and hiding behind
the trees at this very moment——"

Before he could finish his sentence or prepare
for the unexpected movement, Angus started to

his feet, and swinging round his fatal bill-hook, cried out in terror, " Keep off! keep off! or I'll be the death of more than one of you. Let us fight it out, master, and not be strung up like a couple of dogs to the gallows."

" There is no occasion to be alarmed. No one is near, so sit down and be more of a man for the future."

" It gave me a horrid fright though, for all that, and almost took my breath away when you spoke of the officers that I'm always expecting to come and take up the pair of us."

" The pair of us? and why the pair of us? There is no reason that I know, why I should be taken up because you are, or made responsible for your offence. I cannot bring myself to believe that you would see me suffer because you suffered, but should rather think you would do everything to shield me, and take the whole blame on yourself. One man's life is surely enough to atone for an offence; and I cannot imagine that you would wish to sacrifice me, when it would do no good to yourself."

" Don't, master, don't go speaking in that way, or talk of a man's life as if it could be lost to-day and got again to-morrow. It's not like wind in a bagpipe, that comes and goes, and may be had for asking. It's once and for ever,

master! once and no more! so, if you please,
let's talk of something else."

"I think you mean well," said Ellerton, with-
drawing his hand and unclasping the pistol he
had grasped with a desperate intention, on finding Angus less firm than he expected, "and am
prepared to believe that you desire to serve me
faithfully. I have trust in you but not in others;
and I think it right to tell you to be on your
guard, so that in case you left any evidence of
your guilt behind, you may remove it, and get rid of
anything that might tend to criminate you, were
an inquiry to be made into what has taken place."

"No fear of that, master. Let 'em come and
look; they'll find nothing, and may look till
they're blind before they discover him. There is
only one I have any fear of, master, and who
knows more about it than I could wish."

"Indeed!   And who is that?"

"The Devil, master! He knows about it
fast enough, and saw me do it too, but did not
care to prevent me; for, as I stood waiting,
ready to chop him down as he came out, I felt
a hot puff come across my face, and heard him
whisper to me to make sure and not miss my
aim, while his eyes stood out like a pair of
lamps, and lighted the whole place up as if it
had been on fire."

"Don't talk nonsense; but remember you are a man, and should be above such fancies."

"May be, master, and I don't mean to say I oughtn't; but how am I ,to do it, if the devil will come and sit by me, and talk to me, and keep reminding me of what I have done? I ain't a coward, master; I can fight and take a knock or two as well as the best. But then, you see, that's a different affair altogether, and ain't like death a bit. It would not be so bad if he came at a jump and killed you right off; but to know it is coming, or feel it waiting for you, is more than I can bear, and I don't care who knows it."

"But why—why should you suppose it is either, waiting or expecting you? Death is no more likely to come to you now than at any other time; though come it will some day to all of us—the rich as well as the poor."

"But to be hanged, master! Think of that! What a horrid thing death must be with a rope about your neck, and people hooting at you! It's bad enough to die at the best of times; but on the scaffold it's a dozen deaths in one!"

"Hanging!"

"I never saw it but once, master, but as to forgetting it, I can't. It was a big, tall, bony fellow of a nigger as they hanged after he had

8—2

burnt down a planter's house and murdered his
wife and children. He was a month or more
hiding in the bush, till he was half-starved and
couldn't hold out any longer. So they caught
him, lynched him, and run him up to the branch
of a tree while I stood by and saw them do it:
saw his legs kicking, his black head bent on one
side, and his neck twisted like a hayband ! Oh,
God ! master, to think of what I saw, and then
to think that I may be hanged myself, perhaps ;
or have people talk of me as they talked of him,
and say it served me right for something I had
done almost as bad as him !"

"Why do you think of it then? It does not
follow that because they hanged him you are to
be hanged. Your offence is very different. He
murdered women and children ; you revenged
your master, and killed a man who had done
everything in his power to injure him."

"That may be good for niggers, master, but
not for Christians. I said as much before, only
you would not listen to me, but made me do it
whether I liked it or not."

"You said as much before! What do you
mean ?"

"Don't you remember, master, when you
came, a night or two before it happened, and
knocked me up, and told me to get into bed

again while you talked to me of something you wanted me to do ?"

" Oh, yes, I remember."

" And don't you recollect how cold it was, and how you sat upon the bed and tried to persuade me to take the law into my own hands and knock him on the head ? Oh, how I wish it had been only talking, master, and that we two could lay our heads upon our pillows and sleep as we can never hope to sleep again !"

" It's done, and can't be undone. It's no use talking of the past, so let it rest, and think of something else."

" The room was dark as pitch; that I remember well enough; and that you were angry with me because I begged you to think twice, and not ask me to do what I trembled to think about. You would not listen to me, but said, if I would not, you'd get some one else to serve you, whose life you had not saved, and who would prove his love without making the fuss I did about it. ' *I* love you, master,' I called out; ' I love you, and will go through fire and water for you !' ' Prove it then,' said you, ' and do not let me have to think the worse of the world through you, or speak of gratitude as a thing unknown.' I could not bear the thought of that. I wanted to be a good and faithful ser-

vant, but you would not let me! I wanted to
be a Christian and a man, but no! You would
not be content. Nothing but doing what you
wished would do; and so I did it! Hid among
the trees till he came out; as you said he would
as soon as they heard you come—then, with a
sudden swing, lifted up my billhook, and felled
him like an ox!"

"And did you—did you kill him?" said Ellerton, anxious to know, yet trembling to be informed of the particulars of the crime.

"Not that time, master; for he writhed, and
groaned, and tried to speak, so to put him out
of his misery I gave him another blow or two,
and then all was over!"

"And then—what then? Did you carry him
away and throw him in the river?"

"I don't know that I did just then, I was too
frightened to think of anything, and had half
a mind to run away and leave him where he
was. I turned to run, but could not. I was
sick and faint, felt all on fire and then as cold as
ice; but thinking of you, master, I came to a
bit, and fearing you should be suspected, I
dragged him away, worked all night digging at
a hole, then threw him in, and went back to throw
some dust about the place to soak up the stains,
so that no one might know what had taken place."

" But where—where did you bury him ?"

" Don't speak so loud, master, or he may hear you."

" Is he so near us then ?" said Ellerton, looking uneasily about.

" Just under our feet, master; you're treading on him now."

Had the dead man risen through the ground, or sprung up and faced him and taxed him with his death, Ellerton could not have looked more horror stricken, or started back more suddenly from the spot Angus pointed to, as if to indicate the exact place where he was buried.

Was he so near him then that he could have turned the clay up with a spade and exposed him to the light ? . Was he, whom he had set Angus on to kill, lying there indeed, while he had been sitting talking over his grave, and setting his feet upon it ? It was too horrible to be believed; and nothing in the world would have tempted him to remain there, but a fear more dreadful still—that Angus might be tempted to betray him.

" He's safe enough, master, so you need not look so frightened; and ain't likely to get out, unless we drag this log away which I managed to roll over to keep him down."

The picture of those two men talking of their crime, and differently affected by their sense of fear, was one of nature's pictures, and might be studied to advantage by those who desire to paint after her. The one sitting on the log and looking at his feet, the other shrinking and turning from the spot, while the scant rays of light coming through the trees, fell on their figures, and made them stand out forcibly against the darker background lying buried in the gloom.

Were their thoughts as dark and heavy as that gloom, or varied by a sense of fear? The one affected by superstitious dread, the other by doubts as to his personal safety, and ready to seize on any desperate means to free himself from his abhorred association in a deed of blood —as he first drew back a pace, thrust his hand into his pocket, then paused, and gazing on the other said slowly, but as if resolved what to do—

" I have trusted you with my life, I will trust you still; and though I could easily relieve myself of all fears respecting you, I prefer to trust you, and will never conceive it possible that, however you might be tempted to betray me, you would abuse your trust, or sacrifice me to save yourself. I do not think you would. I think better of you, and shall never raise the question in my mind again, nor doubt you, let the consequences be what they may."

" It's very kind of you to say so, master, and kinder still to treat me as you do. You don't look at a man's jacket, master, you want to know what's under it, and if his heart's in the right place. Not like this one down here! He had a fine outside, perhaps, and nothing under it. So has a snake, that you'd put your heel upon and crush, or chop in two, and so get rid of, if you found it in your way."

But Ellerton had heard enough, and, not wishing to listen any longer, he had turned as if to go, when Angus called him back, and taking a button from his pocket rubbed it on his sleeve, then holding it out, said—

"Talking of jackets, master, reminds me of something I found sticking in the grass the other day when I was coming to sit on the log and have a good look to see if all was quiet as I left it."

"Well, what was it?" said Ellerton, coming back, and not too well pleased at having to return.

"I was walking along and thinking, you know of what, when I saw something lying on the ground, which at first I couldn't quite make out, so I picked it up, and found it was a button, as I suppose had been torn off his coat as I dragged him along, and never noticed it all the times I have come out here to sit upon the log and stare down at my feet."

"Throw it away, burn it, or bury it; drive it

with your heel into the ground, and never let me hear you talk again of anything reminding me of that night !"

" It's almost a pity, master; but since you wish it, why away it goes, and mayn't be found so easy as it was. It's a pity, as I said before, but can't be helped, so there's an end of that."

Ellerton waited for no more, but hurrying off left Angus to resume his seat, and before he had time to show him what would still further have excited his horror and alarm had he stayed a little longer to listen to what he had to say.

" It's lucky perhaps that master did not see it, or he might have wanted me to throw this away as well," said Angus, carefully replacing what he held in his hand in his pocket. " I shouldn't like to lose this, for it's something that may turn out handy, and serve to hold a thing or two in. I wonder where the button went ? Somewhere out here, for it hit against that tree and bounded back. I wonder if I could find it if I looked for it?"

After a search among the leaves and grass, he regained the button, rubbed it on his sleeve, then placing it in that something handy which he had wished to show to Ellerton, he went back to his seat on the log of the tree, and steadfastly looking at the ground appeared indifferent to anything else.

CHAPTER VII.

CAPTAIN CONROY NUBBLETON was a man of his word. He was a gentleman, and expected to be treated as a gentleman by those with whom he had the honour of agreeing or differing, as the case might be. He had challenged Mr. Ellerton. He had thrown down the gauntlet, and if he refused to take it up, why he was just the person to post him, or lay his little stick across his shoulders the first time he met him.

The Green Dragon had been his head quarters for the last few weeks, and at the Green Dragon he expected and hoped that Mr. Ellerton's friend would inquire for him, and arrange a meeting with his principal. He had not been there. He had not even called with a view to an amicable settlement of their difference (not that Conroy desired an amicable settlement), but would infinitely have preferred an exchange of shots at six paces, or an encounter with the small sword at but a pace between the two, and was quite at a loss what to make of it.

Sufficient time had elapsed, abundance of time,

had Mr. Ellerton felt the inclination to accept his challenge—but he evidently did not. He was a mean, contemptible coward ; and the gallant Captain was prepared to brand him, and nail him like a bad shilling, for his sneaking, paltry conduct, to every inn-gate in the town.

Not wishing to communicate the cause of his chagrin to his friend and companion, he took pen and paper to his bedroom and wrote to Mr. Ellerton to remind him of his engagement, expressed his regret at the delay that had taken place, and lamented that on an affair of honour it should be necessary to call his attention to the fact that he had not sent his friend to wait on him in answer to his challenge, or complied with the usages of society as a gentleman should do.

The missive despatched, Captain Conroy Nubbleton felt more at ease. He had done everything in his power to stir up his antagonist, but if he would not be stirred up, why there was nothing left for it but a slash, or a kick, and a general expression of indignation against a man who could neglect the courtesy usually recognised in military circles on occasions of this sort.

It happened rather unfortunately that at the time the letter reached its destination, Ellerton was busy perusing another letter and cogitating over its contents, so that when the Captain's missive was handed to him, and after he had glanced at it, he threw it in the fire and left poor Conroy and his anger to expire in the grate.

One letter got rid of, he had a better opportunity of paying attention to the other, which caused him more uneasiness than he expected, since it conveyed to him the intelligence that his brother's son was alive, and could be brought forward to establish his claim at a day's notice.

The letter was addressed from Mr. Blissett's office, and was to all intents and purposes a legitimate communication from a highly respectable firm, so that he paid greater attention, and ceased to look upon it as an attempt to impose upon him, which he had at first taken it to be, and written with a view to extort money from him.

His brother had left a son, so the gipsy told him, though he did not know what had become of him, or if he were dead or alive. If old Daniel had spoken truth—and there was no reason to suppose he had not—that son had by some mysterious means found out the secret of his birth, and was evidently prepared to enforce his claim to the estate as his father's heir. It was no new fear. He had been haunted by it ever since he first heard of his existence, and now that the announcement was made that he was not only alive but represented by a legal firm, he knew the end had come, and that he must either acknowledge him, or dispute his claim by every agency in his power.

It was of no use blinding himself to the true state of affairs or shrinking from the necessity of immediate action. The letter admitted of no delay. It was precise, though courteous. There was no attempt to take advantage of him. It was a plain statement as between client and attorney, but evidenced an intention to proceed for the recovery of the property and estate, should the claim be proved valid in point of law.

What was he to do, tormented and harassed as he was by a thousand fears, not only for the security of his life but the secrecy of one on whom he chiefly depended for his safety? He had no time for reflection, no opportunity for consulting friends, if friends he had, and nothing left but to go up to town, inquire into the true state of affairs, and leave his house unprotected against the designs of those who he had good reason to suppose, would avail themselves of his absence to prosecute inquiry, and tempt his servant to betray him.

His wife too! But he dared not think of her! He knew the illegality of his proceedings, and dreaded the consequences of being dis-covered. He had no time to arrange respecting her, or to place her beyond the reach of help; but must either go off at once to find out who this claimant was, or quietly submit to let proceedings take their course against him.

One thing he dwelt upon with some degree of earnestness, and in which he felt a confidence in the midst of his gravest doubts. It was the secret Daniel had whispered to him respecting the register of birth and the certificate of marriage having been stolen from him, together with the leather pouch in which he kept them. They were powerless to act unless they could produce these or copies of the originals. Should they not be able to do that, they had no legal evidence to go upon, and could easily be defeated in any attempt to enforce their claim for restitution of his father's property and estate.

There were other evidences as well: facts to be proved and traces of his brother to be found, before they could maintain their client's cause, or expect to turn him out to make room for him. That was not so easily done. He would fight it inch by inch, and never consent to abandon his position or yield his right unless compelled to do so, or unless the law should decide against him, and acknowledge his nephew's right in preference to his own.

But the communication must be acted on at

once or treated with indifference. He had to make up his mind, and taking up the letter he read it again.

"Barnard's Inn, July 14, 1835.

"Sir,—I think it necessary to inform you that a person of the name of Daniel Bostock has consulted us upon a subject of considerable importance to you and your interests.

"He states that you have no legal right to the property you hold, but that the son of an elder brother is alive, who can be proved to be his legitimate descendant, and consequently the heir-at-law to the freehold property and estates of Arthur Ellerton the elder. He is a stranger to me, but I have some reason to know that my father is acquainted with him, and has been frequently consulted by him on former occasions. As my father is unfortunately prevented coming to office, in consequence of an accident, I think myself justified in communicating this information to you, so that in the event of our receiving instructions to enforce the claim (provided it can be made out to our satisfaction), you may not be taken at a disadvantage, or complain of want of courtesy on the part of

"Your obedient Servant,

"Pro WILLIAM BLISSETT.

"LEONARD BLISSETT."

There was nothing to take exception to in the wording of the letter, and Ellerton was forced to admit, that much as he had disliked the younger Blissett on first meeting him, his conduct on the present occasion was gentlemanly and proper. He had left nothing to be explained hereafter, but by informing him beforehand of what might ultimately happen, had prepared him to anticipate the enforcement of a claim, which, could it be shown to be reasonably conclusive, they, the Blissetts, would be bound to proceed in, if instructed to do so by a sufficiently responsible client.

It was important that he should see the younger Mr. Blissett immediately, ascertain if any legal claim could be made on the estate, who the claimant was, and if the Mr. Bostock mentioned in the letter had really been empowered to assert his rights, or was simply an adventurer anxious to make capital out of a presumed knowledge of the secrets of his family. The advertisements might have set him on to imagine that an advantage could be gained by bringing forward some one as the supposed heir, and that that some one was a willing party in the scheme, if he only got well paid for it, and were held harmless of consequences.

As no time was to be lost, he left Angus in

charge of the house, and particularly enjoined on him the necessity of keeping a careful watch, not only on the house but on those who might invent excuses for coming to it, either on pretence of inquiring for him, or asking questions about his wife. He was to refuse admittance to every one, keep a constant guard, and above all, to be sure and hold his tongue on matters relating to himself, his wife, and family.

The coach was changing horses at the Red Lion, as he took his seat inside, and he flattered himself that by catching the coach the moment it came up, he had escaped observation, and hoped to find all things as he had left them, and safe in charge of Angus, by the time he returned.

But before the coach had fairly got to London, and Ellerton could hope to discover what he went for, or find out Leonard Blissett—a change had taken place which so entirely altered his position, he might have saved himself the trouble, and remained at home for any good he got by it. His absence was the one thing chiefly wished for, and looked forward to. It was what was wanted and desired, and before he came back, Jane and her friends had seized the opportunity and made the best use of it, as he found to his cost.

CHAPTER VIII.

BIRTHS, DEATHS, AND MARRIAGES.

THE roadside inn, to which Mr. Blissett had been carried after his accident, was snug and comfortable. The doctor had shown unusual ability, and as Mrs. Blissett had been sent for to nurse him and attend to his comforts, he did not find the confinement so irksome, as at first sight it had threatened to be.

In less than a month he was on his legs again ; weak, of course, but in good spirits, anxious to get to London to look after business, and get through the pile of work he knew had accumulated since his illness, and which must be attended to without loss of time the moment he could stir about and set things to rights.

He stood the journey tolerably well, and on arriving in town was better than could have been expected. Still he had to keep the house for a day or two, and to submit to the doctor's orders, so that he missed the opportunity of welcoming his friend in the drab great-coat and Glengarry cap, as he walked up Barnard's Inn the day after his return, and thrusting his head in at the office

9—2

door, inquired with his usual burr, if the "governor" was in.

The "governor" was not in, but the young
governor was, and as Mr. Bostock made no
objection, but seemed to prefer the young governor to the old one, he sent in a message by the
clerk to say that a gentleman, well known to his
father, wished to see Mr. Blissett junior on important business.

Before the clerk could take in his name, the
Northumbrian was on his heels, and, brushing
past, he pushed into the room before him, not only
to the surprise of Leonard, but of the clerk, who
was about saying something sharp, when Mr.
Bostock shut the door in his face, and told him
to go downstairs, as he was not wanted; then,
nodding to Leonard, sat down, and introduced
himself and business without further preface.

"So you ca' this a la'yer's office, do you?
An' a pretty web it is in which to catch the flies
an' suck 'em dry as sawdust. There's no much
left in 'em, I tack it, a'ter you've had the squeez-
ing of 'em, an' deil a ha'p'orth to spare, I
reckon, gude, bad, or indifferent, when you've
done wi' 'em."

"If, sir," said Leonard, annoyed by Mr.
Bostock's uncouth manner, yet willing to take
his bluntness in good part—"you have no

further business here than to express your
sentiments upon law and lawyers, the better
thing would have been to avoid connexion with
them, and not thrust yourself where you were
not asked, and certainly were not wanted."

"Eh! but you're right there. It's not so
intimate I am with you as wi' the old gentleman, an' not so weel known to you as I am to
him. But, if I don't mistack, I have seen you
aince before, upon the doorstep, when the Captain—as the leddy ca'd him—war talking grand
an' mighty, an' had weel nigh got a souse on the
chops for glavering of what he'd do wi' his wee
bit cane about my shoulders."

" I remember the meeting to which you refer,
and my surprise at finding you and my father
closeted together when I went upstairs, after
putting the lady and the Captain into a coach."

" Oh, she war a rum 'um, she war ; scranny
as a threadpaper, an' him plucky as a sparrow.
It's Long Acre an' Little S'Martin's Lane, an' a
bad match, anyhow, as fur as sizes go."

" As that is a matter interesting to them, and
not to us, I must beg of you to confine yourself
to any business communication you may have to
make, and dispense with comparisons on the lady
or her friend."

" Wi' all my heart, altho' meeting them here

was somewhat of the oddest, a'ter the upset we
had together in the coach, when they tumbled
on the top o' me, an' thumped me black an'
blue.   It's not so easy to forget the digs an'
scratches I got down there, an' how my bonnet
war mashed, an' pounded almaist, by their
elbows an' their knees."

"I am glad to see it has recovered its shape,
and that you are so well satisfied with it, you
make a point of keeping it on your head, when
gentlemen usually take off *their* hats on coming
into a room."

"A bonnet's a bonnet! it's not a het; an'
may be worn on a man's head in the presence of
a king.   That is, a bonnet that's a gude bonnet,
and not some mackbelieve thing or other, that's
no more like a Paisley bonnet than a shilling's
like a guinea."

"Pray reserve to yourself the pleasure of the
distinction, and favour me with your business.
If it is anything with which my father is especially acquainted, or if you wish to benefit by
his personal advice, I regret to inform you that
you will have to wait until he is sufficiently recovered from his accident to be well enough to
attend to the duties of office."

"Met wi' an accident, has he ?   Of course
he did.   Weel it can't be helped.   But as it's

you, not him, I want this time, I shan't be
worritted with a disappointment at not seeing
him, anyhoo."

Disgusted with the fellow's selfishness and
utter disregard to the suffering of others,
Leonard was on the point of expressing himself
warmly, when the north countryman prevented
him, and launched at once into the subject of his
visit, and the occasion of his seeking him at Barnard's Inn.

"You see," he said, "it's been a long time
coming about, an' it's no so easy a matter as people
think for a man to mack up his mind to spend a
lot o' brass on the chance of findin' out some one,
who mayn't, a'ter all, be so grateful as he should
be for my hunting up a fortune for him."

"Perhaps," replied Leonard, utterly indifferent
as to whether the north countryman met his
reward or not, and indeed scarcely thinking of
what he said.

"It's not 'perhaps;' it's downright positive;
an' the thought can't be lifted off a man's mind
so easy as you think. It's a lump of lead on
the top of him; an' it war through looking a'ter
that as brought the Captain an' the leddy down
on me, as I said before, when they lay kicking
at the bottom of the lang-stage coach, an' nearly
spoilt my bonnet."

" Well—well ?"

" It war not ' weel'. It war wrang an' bad, an' a mercy I survived, an' war no carried in a hearse to the Cas'le, instead of a post-sha', to satisfy mysel whether Mother Savaker were the same Poll Woodruff as aince upon a time hoed an' stubbed on Black Acre Farm, as belongs to my uncle Thomas."

" What in the name of fortune, my good sir, has all this to do with me ? or in what way can Poll Woodruff, or Mother Savaker as you call her, be brought to bear on the business which brings you here ?"

" It's not the outside of the nut you must judge of. You must crack an' try afore you can say it's gude or bad ; not that I mean to say that Mother Savaker an't a hard 'un to crack. She is ! You might as weel tack a bite at a stane as at her, an' mack your jaws ache, afore you could mack her motherly an' kind to the lost son I war in search of."

" Oh, it is *her* son then whose fortune you hope to make, and who is to reward you for finding it out, is it ?"

" I didna' say just that, but as it is in professional confidence, I may as weel save a deal of beating about the bush by confessing it at aince. Weel, then, we'll say it war her son, an' that he had been lost sight of sin' he war a child, an' might as weel not have been born for anything she cared for him, or anyone else cared for him, at all times excepting Dan Bostock, who is the only friend he has in the world."

"If he pays him well," put in Leonard.

"Of course.   It's no so pleasant to work for nought, an' get kicked an' tossed about as I have been, except on a remunerative principle.   Ten p' cent. upon the whole is what I look to get, else, may the deil fly away wi me if I don't leave him a beggar all his life, instead of proving him heir to a fine property."

"To his mother's pots and pans, I suppose, or the goodwill of the Castle," said Leonard, laughing.

"It's no to pots an' pans he is heir, but to a fine estate that's worth a thousand goodwills an' a thousand Castles tumbled into one.   It's a langsome story, but as we're in for it, I may as weel have it out, an' then you'll be able to advise the young man what he should do, provided I can mack out his title, an' establish his claim."

"I am at your service, pray proceed."

"Weel, aince upon a time, a certain somebody fell in love wi' our Poll.   She war a strapping wench, with wonderful black eyes, an' war reckoned a beauty in a rough way.   There war a dozen or more had a mind to her, but only this

one who had the misfortune (as I may ca' it).
to please her, an' like a fool marry her."

" Was she such a terrible vixen then?"

. " A vixen! weel, weel, we'll ca' it vixen an'
you like, though Poll war more like a wild cat
when her tongue were set agoing, an' her eyes
dancing in her hed; than anything else.   It's
not so easy a thing to pacify an angry woman
at the best o' times.   But Poll warn't to be
pacified at any time; she war a downright fury!
so her husband made a bolt of it, an' ran away
from her, as I have heard."

" And it was a child by this marriage——"

" A poor misused, graceless little varmint; a
heavy clumpy child, that the mother could not
bear the sight of, though the father did.   So he
took it wi' him, an' left Marm Poll to storm an'
rage, an' swear she'd be the death of him if she
catched him."

" But how can this child (providing you could
trace him) be made to be the heir to the fine
estate you talk about?   Was his father a landed
proprietor, or his mother heiress to Black Acre
Farm?"

" Gin you'll only be patient you'll find what
he war heir to, an' hoo his title can be made
gude to the satisfaction of the law.   Now Poll's
husband war a lazy chap; he knew no trade, an'

- never could be got to work at anything, but would keep idling about, an' come an' go just as he pleased, an' leave his wife to keep the pot boiling as best she could. So that you see, though Poll war a spitfire, she had some reason for her tantrums, there's no doubt o' that."

"From what I hear," said Leonard, "I am inclined to pity the woman. But if her husband knew no trade, how came she to marry him?"

"You must ax her yourself there. She had a woman's reason I'll be bound, an' would most likely say he war a tall, handsome man, an' superior to the louts she had met with. But it war hinted that he war a gentleman in disguise, an' that our Poll might some day turn out a leddy, if she only behaved hersel, though he did go about as a gipsy."

"A gipsy!"

"So I heard, an' the laziest vagabond you'd find in a day's march. Now it war owing to his being thought to be a gipsy, an' to some one telling Poll he war, that set her on to find him out a'ter he had left her for a year or two, or more."

"She found him then, at last?"

"Weel, no! I can't exactly say she did. But she heard of him, an' that he had died soon a'ter he left her. She heard another thing as

weel, which war, that though he had married her
in the name of Reuben Craddock, it war not his
right name, but that he war a gentleman's son
in downright earnest, who had left his father's
hoose to join a set of vagabonds he ought to
have been ashamed of."

"What proof have you of this?"

"Plenty of proof! bushels of proof, you may
tack my word for it, or I wouldn't have been
such a gowk as to spend my money in ferretting
him out. Weel, this war hard news for Poll, for
though she never let him have a moment's peace
when he war alive, she took on sadly a'ter he
war dead, an' vowed she would never marry anybody else. A kindness on her part that spoke
weel for her charity, an' I hope war taken
account of by the men in the neighbourhood."

"But the child?"

"Oh, he war safe enough, but war about as
idle a young vagabond as you ever see, an' as
like his father as one peasward is like another.
Now the boy war a heavy, sleepy boy, an' having
had a taste of gipsy life, he wanted to keep to
it. But Poll would no' ha' it; so she bundled
him off, took him over the Border, an' got him a
service wi' an honest old couple who took a
liking to him, an' wanted to adopt him, to supply
the place of a son they had lost."

" And this child you would wish to show has an interest in some property or other with which you are acquainted ?"

" That's just it.   I war put on the scent by reading an advertisement in a newspaper, an' as I happened to know something about it, I thou't I might find out more, an' grab the reward, as weel as the payment I might receive from the grateful heir in return for my services. But when I came to look for him, he war gone ! gone off to Jamaica years before, an' nothing known what had become of him from the time he went away."

" To Jamaica ?"

" So they said, an' that he had been a sore trouble to the puir boddies, who finding he would no' wark, nor do anything to earn his bread, sent him out wi' a factor just starting from the neighbourhood to try what foreign parts could do for him.   This war a slap in the face I didna' expect, so I made up my mind to wash my hands of the business, an' stomach my loss as I would a stane.   But I war no satisfied.   I war savage at being baulked, an' as I happened to hear that our Poll had broken her word, an' married again, I thou't I'd find her out.   An' sure enough I did; fund her at the Castle at Newark, a'ter she had put an end to the exciseman by her tantrums, who left her sole mistress of all he war worth."

" And what did you do then ?"

" E'en broke my shins over her, and had to stand her bullyragging because I bought a pint of yell an' a munch of bread an' cheese in a street off by, an' did no pay twa shillings for a supper at the Cas'le. This made her stomachy ; she wud no say a word about the boy, but blazed out at me at such a rate, because I took a squint at her in her bar parlour, I thou't I saw the old exciseman tremble in his frame, an' turn the colour of a blue-bag at the sound of her voice."

" And so you gave up further seeking ; kept your money and——"

" There you're wrang. In for a penny, in for a pund, you know. So I thou't I'd have another shy, an' ruinate mysel entirely. Walked to Bristol, bargained for a steerage passage to Jamaica, an' nearly lost my bonnet in a sudden blaw of wind."

" That would have been a misfortune," said Leonard with a laugh.

" Weel, I got out to Jamaica, after a fearfu' passage, but had better ha' stayed at hame, for on making inquiries, I fund that he had gone back to England only the week before, on board the

Nancy, an' so a' my trouble an' expense war thrown away."

"It was a disappointment, I confess," said Leonard, secretly enjoying the Northumbrian's distress.

"A disappointment do you ca' it? It war downright spiteful, an' enough to drive a man daft wi' only thinking on it. Think of the brass I had spent—think of my sousing in the spray, an' my discomfits in the fore cabin of a West India trader; blawn by all winds but the right one, an' tossed an' tumbled, like a lemon in a bowl o' punch. Weel, it wud no do to stay out there. It war blazing hot, an' I with nathing but my drab great-coat, frizzling an' frying, an' mysel baking in it like a dish of hotch-potch in an oven! I had not lang to wait. What went out badly came hame weel, an' though we pitched an' tossed a bit, we got to Bristol safely, where I landed with a lasting recollection of the pleasures of the sea; smelling of molasses like a sugar hogshead, an' fumigated wi' rum like a dram shop."

"And when you got to Bristol?" said Leonard, with difficulty repressing his laughter.

"Oh, it's no laughing matter," replied the Northumbrian, "but the risk of a man's life, which ought to be thou't of by a grateful heir, an'

rewarded handsomely.   But as you say, I got to
Bristol ; an' what then ? Why, then I had to dodge
au' poke about, ax questions, an' get cross answers,
until I fund out the owners of the *Nancy*, who
told me that she war wracked an' foundered !
an' gone. down like a bucket in a well !   Just
think o' that noo, an' then say hoo you would
ha' liked it yoursel ?"

" Well, I must say you had enough to try
your patience."

" Patience ! I war downright wild, an' might
ha' gone out o' my senses, had I not heard that
one of the puir critters had been saved an'
rescued by a miracle !"

" And that one ?"

" The lad himsel ! Think o' that noo ! Saved
by a merciful Providence, as I may almost say,
on purpose to pay me back my brass.   It war
weel known who had rescued him, an' hoo, by
another merciful Providence, the very man who
should a' wished him drowned, had picked him
out o' the sea, an' saved him to turn him out of
his estate, for he war no other than the rightful
heir of Reuben Craddock, otherwise Arthur
Ellerton."

" Arthur Ellerton !"

" Eh ? I thou't I should startle you, an' you'll
not say noo that I wasted your time for naething.

It's a plain matter of fact, I tell you, an' if you've twa eyes in your hed, you'll see your way to it as plain as a toad in a hole."

"You have made out a tolerably good case, I own," said Leonard, after a pause, "but it will require careful investigation before we can move in it. Mr. Ellerton is a man of property, and from what I hear, has succeeded to his estate in default of a more immediate heir, but after diligent inquiry had been made to discover him. Now, what I want to ask is, have you informed my father of this matter, and is he acquainted with what you have explained to me? I imagine that such must be the case, as he appeared to have some previous knowledge of you, and that you consulted him before consulting me."

"Naething of the sort. He knows no more than Adam what I have fund out; an' ain't likely, unless I tell him. You see, my brother is a la'yer out in Alnwick, an' it war through him I first came to ferret out a claim, which, strange to say, upsets your own, an' will bother the old governor considerably about Poll Woodruff and her son."

"Poll Woodruff! What can he know of her, and how can any claim of mine be jeopardized through her, or by any son of hers?" said Leonard, with a stare.

"What will you gi' me noo to hold my tongue? What will you gi' me to burn the documents I have in my pocket, an' forget hoo I searched an' tumbled over the leaves of the register of births, an' marriages, an' deaths in that old church out on the Border, where I kept the parson waiting in the vestry till he war shivering wi' cold, spelling the names over in the buke."

"What will I give?" said Leonard, utterly confounded by Mr. Bostock's proposition, and equally at a loss in applying a meaning to his words.

"Oh, I am no so difficult to comprehend, though you mack believe as if I war. I am open to an offer—a substantial and reasonable offer, I mean; an' the moment the brass is paid, I will tack my affidavy to keep a' snug an' quiet, an' hand you over the certificate of marriage an' the certificate of birth which Arthur Ellerton gave for safe keeping into the charge of an old gipsy, an' which the old vagabond kept for years in an old leather pouch, till he war robbed of it, an' could not hand it over when it war wanted."

"If so, how came they in your possession?"

"Oh, that's easy enough made out. I bought the documents of a gipsy thief of a fellow, who, for aught I know, may have stunned the old man first, an' picked his pocket a'terwards. That's no business of mine, you know. I got what I wanted, but not the pouch. That he war afeard to part wi' perhaps, though I saw it, an' could swear to it anywhere, for it had a rusty steel clasp to it, an' war made of a bit o' hide, an' full of odds an' ends which the old man kept in it; such as a silver ring, a tobacco-stopper, a child's caul, an' his old wife's tooth."

" Will you let me look at them ? I mean the certificate of marriage and the copy of the register of birth. The tooth and the child's caul you had better keep, in case you should have to make another voyage, and wish to provide against contingencies."

Mr. Bostock, upon this, took out his pocket-book, and carefully selecting the documents referred to, spread them on the table. He made a clumsy sort of excuse for keeping his hands on them, by pretending that great care must be taken of them, and contrived it so that while Leonard followed the direction of his finger, he still retained possession of them, to prevent the possibility of their being destroyed.

The certificate of marriage was a discoloured piece of paper, dirty and worn; but the writing was legible, and certified that on August 15th,

1804, Reuben Craddock, bachelor, had married Mary Woodruff, spinster. The certificate was signed by the officiating clergyman, and Leonard read with some surprise, the name of William Arkwright, curate, as the attesting witness.

Now the name of Reuben Craddock, as Mr. Bostock pointed out, could be shown to be the one Arthur Ellerton assumed after he left his father's house, and joined the tribe of gipsies with whom he subsequently took up his abode. There were a dozen or more of the tribe who could swear to that, as he said, and also that he always went by that name during the time he lived with them; that he was married in that name, and buried in it, as could be proved incontestably.

"I think noo," said the Northumbrian, after he had suffered Leonard to read the certificate of birth, which set forth that on July 29th, 1805, Arthur, son of Reuben Craddock and Mary his wife, had been baptised in the same church, and been christened by the same clergyman—"I have pretty weel established my position, as you will see by these certified copies I got extracted from the register, signed by Ernest Arkwright, a nephew of the old curate, who is the rector noo, while this one is curate under him, an' biding his time to slip into his shoes."

"But what is this?" said Leonard, glancing at another paper folded with the others. "This appears to be the certificate of another birth, and of another son born to the same parties."

"Eh—that has slippit in where it had no right to go, an' war' not meant to be exhibited just at present. You see it war the advertisements as did it; an' as my brother happened aince upon a time to be a witness to a sort o' agreement between certain parties—who shall be nameless —about adopting a puir laddie, while he war serving his articles at Alnwick—why he took a copy of it, do ye see, an' like a carefu' man, kept it in case something should happen to mack his information valuable."

"Oh, indeed!" said Leonard. "I imagine that carefulness is a distinguishing characteristic in your family, and not likely to be lost sight of while Mr. Daniel Bostock lives."

The Northumbrian acknowledged the compliment by a nod, then went on to say—

"Now as Ellerton war the name buzzed about our parts, in consequence of some gipsy chap who war sweet on Poll—telling her that that war her husband's proper name—my brother made a note of it, an' when the advertisement came out, we agreed to go snacks in the reward if I fund out the lad through what he told me.

But, by good luck, I war put on a wrong scent, an' kept floundering on till I discovered that Poll had had twa sons, an' that the elder one war the one I wanted, not the one my brother meant."

"Then your brother's share——"

"An't worth that," said the Northumbrian, snapping his fingers. "This one is my awn findin', an' if he gets a brass farden out of the reward, why, the grateful heir may pay it himsel, so there's an end o' that."

Mr. Bostock had evidently had his say, and it only remained for Leonard to accept the business or decline it. In neither case did he feel himself warranted to act without first consulting his father, but as he had certain reasons just then operating in his mind in reference to Mr. Ellerton, he spoke the Northumbrian fairly; promised to lay a statement of the case before a competent authority, and dismissed him on the understanding that he should hear from him as soon as he had determined what to do, and made himself master of the whole affair.

Acquainted with Mr. Bostock's amiable views, and possessed to the full extent of his desires, yet anxious to act with strict professional propriety, Leonard Blissett perhaps exceeded its necessity when he resolved to write to Ellerton,.

and inform him that the heir to his father's estate had been discovered.

He had another reason.   But for that Bertha must be answerable ; and, perhaps, the writers of the communications he constantly received, informing him of certain matters discussed in secret in the recesses of the " Green Dragon."

CHAPTER IX.

THE OLD POST-CHAISE.

LEONARD's letter had had the desired effect. It had tempted Ellerton to quit his home, and leave it in the charge of Angus, at a time that it was dangerous to have quitted it under any circumstances, for Jane, who was always on the watch, saw him leave by the little park-gate, and carrying his valise and cloak, as if starting on a journey.

As it was important that she should find out where he went and what he was doing, she ran out after him, but unfortunately missed him, and did not arrive in time even to see the coach before it started.

But Jane had a tongue in her head, and as she knew that the ostler at the " Red Lion " was dying for her, and would do anything to please her, she crossed the road, looked delighted at seeing him, though she hated him, and wished him good morning with a smile that would have melted a heart of ice.

The effect was instantaneous! Down went the horse-clothes in a heap, up went the wet leather to his face, and left it shining like a coach-panel!

Jane blushed, the ostler grinned, and the stable helps began laughing, to her great annoyance.

But as she had to find out something, she submitted to be winked and grinned at, spoke timidly and softly, and asked the ostler " if he knew whether Mr. Ellerton had gone to London in the coach ?"

" Just started, Miss," replied the ostler. " Took a inside place as if it was in a hearse, and looked as black as thunder cos I touched my head and said 'Good morning, sir.' How you can stand his looks, and put up with what you meets at that house, is wonderful to me, when you knows as well as I do that there's about as snug a couple of rooms over the stables as ever you see, as you might be missus of at any time, if you only said the word."

" Thank you," said Jane; " much obliged to you, I am sure, but I'll trouble you not to talk stuff of that sort to me, or I'll box your ears."

Before the ostler could recover his surprise, or polish up his face with another rub, Jane was off, and running towards the outskirts of the town, arrived at the " Green Dragon " just as the two gentlemen were sitting down to breakfast, and prepared to do justice to it.

The Captain had been up early as usual, and having waited till he was tired for Mr. Ellerton's reply to his letter, he was in the act of stirring up his cup of coffee, when in rushed Jane, out of breath, and full of the news she had to tell of her master, and of his having gone by the early coach to London.

Not a moment was to be lost. The bell was rung, and a post-chaise ordered to be got ready immediately, as one of the gentlemen had to go to town, and wanted to overtake the coach before it reached its first stage on the road to London.

The " Green Dragon " answered to the call. The chaise was at the door, and the oldest post-boy on the road ready in the saddle before a dozen mouthfuls could be swallowed, when the Rev. Mr. Arkwright took his seat inside, told the old boy to drive like the wind, and promised to reward him handsomely if he overtook the coach in the first ten miles.

The Captain waved his hand, Jane dropped a curtsey, and off rattled the chaise, leaving the landlord and landlady in amazement, and the Captain to order a fresh relay of ham and eggs, and a fresh supply of coffee to finish his breakfast.

What could it all be about? There had been nothing but hurry and confusion ever since the gentlemen had stayed there, and the girl from the big house came to see them at strangely improper hours, and be waited on as if she was a lady, when she was only old Botcherby's daughter, and no better than any other servant in the town. But as the gentlemen paid liberally, and did not seem to be too particular what they paid, why the landlord thought that it might be as well to hold his tongue and behave civilly to her, as a post-chaise had been ordered, no doubt through her, and from something she had said, which had the effect of starting one of the gentlemen to London.

Where the chaise went, or changed horses, is a secret known only to the reverend gentleman, and to the venerable post-boy. It overtook the coach; passed it at the second stage, and rattled into London, where the reverend gentleman took a hackney-coach, drove to Barnard's Inn, and, after a short stay, ordered Jarvie in another direction, and towards the suburbs, where he waited some time; drove back again and took his seat in the post-chaise standing ready to receive him in the inn yard at which it had been put up, when the horses were started off afresh, driven through the Borough on the road to Kent, and smoked along as if Old Nick, instead of the old post-boy, had been driving them.

No sooner had one surprise been got rid of, than there came another! for, on the chaise drawing up at the "Green Dragon"—and after it had performed a journey to London and back in an incredibly short space of time—out stepped, not only the reverend gentleman, but a lady! A lady, by the look of her, and a smart, handsome lady, who shook hands with the Captain, and then went into the inn in company with the two gentlemen, where refreshments were ordered to be got ready, and the chambermaid called to conduct her to a room.

This was taking the "Green Dragon" by surprise, and the landlady grew rather doubtful as to the respectability of the proceedings, and how far it might be prudent to sanction such doings in a steady-going old-fashioned inn, such as the "Green Dragon" had always been known to be! Jane came—but went! But here was a lady, brought all the way from London, shown into one of the best rooms, and invited to join the gentlemen at dinner! The thing was incomprehensible, and the landlady grew nervous thinking that she might stay all night and get the inn talked about, until she remembered that there was only one lady between two gentlemen, and no chance of a second—unless Jane came to make the numbers even.

But the most unexpected thing of all, was the chaise being ordered out again after dinner, and the old boy summoned to get into the saddle to drive the lady somewhere else. It was raining, and threatened to be a bad night; but that made no difference. The chaise must go! And what on earth it all meant the landlady could not comprehend, till she began to think that the gentlemen had some difficulty in agreeing about the lady, or the lady some difficulty in deciding which should be the gentleman.

The post-boy never murmured; never said a word; but got into the saddle and drove off without even asking where to; then, leaving the Captain and his friend looking out after them, turned into the High Street, as if he knew exactly where to go and what to do with the lady, and held his tongue, as he had been told to do.

On roads, through towns, up streets, and ways impossible to be enumerated, that old post-chaise had rattled till one would have thought it had had enough of it! Since eight to eight it had been hard at work, and now it had to bump and creak again, rattle and shake, and thump upon its worn out springs till its framework quivered, while the old plated lamps (the remnants of somebody's grandeur), as if mocking the post-boy, jumped up and down, and jogged, and jogged, and kept a restless motion in their worn-out sockets.

It was not the first time by many, that the old

post-chaise had clattered through the High Street
of that country town, or. its faded yellow body,
and no less faded post-boy, had been recognised
by the oldest inhabitants as familiar friends.
The ostler at the " Red Lion" glanced at it dis-
dainfully ; the stable helps saluted it with a cry
of derision ; even the urchins in the streets yelled .
after it, and made of it a great rejoicing as they
climbed up behind, hurrahed, and cheered, and
by a variety of pleasing attentions exhibited their
pleasure and surprise at seeing that old tumble-
down post-chaise upon the move again, after they
had fancied that it had been chopped up and
burned for firewood a year or more ago.

Had they but known of its successful journey
to London and back all in a day, their wonder
would have been immense ! They would have
left off chasing it, or running by its side, and
hung back awe-struck and confounded by the
novelty of its achievement'! Even the little
ragged rascal perched behind, and who got
hooked upon a spike in getting down—even he
would have left off blubbering when he saw it
turn out of the High Street into the road leading
to " The House" with half his jacket hanging to
it, and borne the thwacking he got when he
went home with magnanimity, if he had only
known of it.

The road to "The House" led by a round-about into the main road some miles farther on. Down this road the post-chaise turned, and was driven to the lodge gates, through which it passed, then keeping along the carriage-drive, proceeded towards the house.

It was getting dark. The drizzle had changed to heavy rain! The sky was dark! The house looked black as ink. There were no lights in the windows, and not a soul to be seen, giving it the appearance of a deserted dwelling, and shut up for good.

As intimately acquainted with the winding of the carriage-drive as if he had been born on it, the post-boy turned, and wound, until he pulled up at the doorway of the house. Ringing the bell and letting down the steps, he handed the lady out, saw her safe under the shelter of the porch, then jerking his horses round, drove off, and made for the outskirts of the town, where he pulled up at the "Green Dragon," and never said a word of where he had been, or what he had done with the lady, but left his mistress to imagine that he had deposited her somewhere, where she had no doubt she would ultimately be found in very bad company.

As the Captain and his friend were naturally anxious to inquire after the lady, and the exact spot to which she had been driven, they went out soon after his return, and on going into the stables found the venerable post-boy dripping to the skin, and wringing out his jacket ; when, no doubt compassionating his watery state, and to prevent his catching cold, the reverend gentleman put something in his hand, which he said would warm him if he only melted a little of it and took it at once.

Whatever that something was need not be told. But he first of all asked change for a sovereign at the bar ; drank a glass of brandy (he did not require water), then went back into the stable to show the gentlemen all about the place, and the identical horses he had driven the first stage out and the last stage in ; pointed to the dilapidated chaise he had driven all his life, but never in all his life had made so good a day's work by, as that day, after the two gentlemen had had a little talk with him, and found out what an excellent old boy he was.

And he was. He proved himself the best of company in the tap-room that night, sang the best song, drank ale when he grew tired of rum-and-water, then took to rum again till he could drink no more, but made a shift to find his way to the stables, where he found the old post-chaise waiting for him, and ready for another run if he only wanted it.

True to his old habit he tried to mount, but as there were no horses, he took an inside place and made himself comfortable : slept like a top, fancied he was being driven by his mistress dressed in his top boots and leathers, and woke with laughing as he thought that he saw her bump and bump, and wished he had slept on, for he wanted more rum, and could not get it.

CHAPTER X.

LEFT under the porchway of Mr. Ellerton's house, and anxious to obtain admittance, the lady the postboy had driven from the inn, was patient, but persevering. Finding no one come to answer her summons, she rang again—rang till the house echoed, and she was tired; and then began to fear that the place was really deserted, and no one left to reply to her inquiries, or relieve her anxiety on a subject she had at heart.

Worn out with waiting, and not knowing what to do, she began to think that she had come to the wrong entrance, and must try somewhere else, even if she had to go out into the rain and seek for it. To remain where she was was hopeless, as there seemed to be no chance of anyone coming to tell her what to do, or to let her in, which was the thing she chiefly desired.

But no; for on going into the rain, and looking up at the house, it struck her as being even more dark and desolate than when seen from the porchway. The grounds were bare and neglected, the flower-beds overgrown with weeds, and the appearance of the place so melancholy and dull, that she was glad to get under the porch again and wait patiently, in hopes her ringing might be heard, and ensure her the night's lodging she so much wished to obtain.

Down poured the rain—the heavy, steep-down rain, that seemed to fall on purpose to make things more wretched still; pattering and falling on the leaves, dripping from the roof in large, round drops, and working up the gravel into holes. But as it was of no use waiting doing nothing, she rang, then listened—listened for the faintest sound of footsteps, or the murmuring of voices, until she thought that the people in the house must be dead, and that she should have to go away and give up all hope of obtaining admittance.

At last, and after she had come to the conclusion that it was of no use waiting any longer listening to the dull pattering of the rain, and the heavy drips still falling from the house, she thought she heard a buzz of voices, and then footsteps, as if people were stirring in the place, and coming to inquire what she wanted.

She could hear them more distinctly after a time, and that one voice was high and shrill, the other low and soft. They were voices anyhow—human voices, and not the wild, unearthly shrieks

11—2

she had half expected to hear ring through the place, and startle her to fancy that it was some poor maniac fighting for her liberty and struggling to get free.

She heard the people inside talking now, and one endeavouring to persuade the other to open the door, and that other vowing she would not. The low, soft voice entreating, while the person with the shrill one answered sharply, and spoke angrily in reply, though after a time she appeared to relent, for the door was slowly opened, when the lady found herself face to face with the old housekeeper and her daughter Jane.

"Who may you please to want," inquired Mrs. Botcherby, seeing a lady waiting in the porch. "If it's master, he's away, and wont be back before to-morrow night."

"Pray don't shut the door, you dear good soul, for I am half perished standing out here in the cold waiting for you to let me in."

"Who said I was going to ·let you in? I didn't, and shouldn't think of such a thing when it's against master's orders, and more than my place is worth to disobey," said Mrs. Botcherby, holding the door, and holding it in such a manner that no one could pass without her permission.

"How you do talk, mother, to be sure," said Jane, coming a little forward. "I should have

thought that you would have had more manners
than to keep a lady waiting in the cold who had
called to see master or mistress. Your place, indeed ! I'll engage to get you a dozen as good, more
comfortable and sociable than the one you have,
even if Mr. Ellerton did turn you off, which ain't
likely, for being civil to one of his friends."

" Don't you be so ready with your tongue,
Miss. I say it's against master's orders to let
anyone in, and I'm not going to disobey them to
please you ; so you may as well learn to behave
yourself, and not talk of what you don't understand."

" But, my dear good soul, what am I to do ?"
urged Bertha. "I can't find my way back to
the town by myself, for it is so dark I shouldn't
know which way to turn, and should get wet
through walking through the rain."

" The same turning that brought you will take
you back, and as you didn't mind the rain in
coming, I don't see why you should care about
it going back," said Mrs. Botcherby, even more
resolutely than before, and keeping possession of
the doorway.

" You don't suppose I walked here, do you, on
a night like this ? I took a carriage at the inn, of
course, and drove here, but not supposing that I
should want it when I came to see my sister——."

" Sister !" half shrieked Mrs. Botcherby.

" I discharged it as soon as I got out, and had no notion that I should be refused admittance because her husband was away, and not expected home at present, which I am very sorry for, as he of course would be much annoyed at the coldness of my reception."

Jane said nothing, but she nodded her head over Mrs. Botcherby's shoulder to Bertha, as much as to say, that she had managed capitally, and had driven her mother into a corner, out of which she would find it difficult to escape.

But the old woman was not yet defeated. She had something more to say, and did not stick at a lie to suit her purpose.

" Sorry to disappoint you, I am sure, Miss; but Mr. and Mrs. Ellerton are abroad, and not expected home for goodness knows when."

There was no getting over this. Bertha could not say that she knew better, and Jane did not dare to contradict her mother for fear of creating suspicion, and making her more obstinate than ever. But she shook her head behind her back, and motioned to Bertha not to believe a word she said, which she didn't.

" Oh, what a dreadful disappointment! Here have I come all the way from London on purpose to stay a week or two with my sister, as she has often wished me, and now that I have come, she has gone abroad without saying a word about it, and Mr. Ellerton, of course, gone with her, so that I am quite bewildered and can't tell what to make of it."

Bertha deserved to be rewarded for her tact. By carefully avoiding mentioning what Mrs. Botcherby had said about Mr. Ellerton's returning the following night, she pretended to be completely deceived by her account of his and her sister's absence from England.

It was a good hint for Jane, and she took up her cue capitally.

"Well, of all the provoking things I ever heard!" said Jane. "Only to think of mistress's sister coming all the way from London, and then to find the house shut up and mistress away. I am heartily sorry, I am sure, Miss, and so is mother, I know; only what are we to do? You see we are only servants here, and can't do what we like, as master has left his man behind to keep us in order, and prevent our doing anything he dislikes."

"Who cares for him, I should like to know?" cried Mrs. Botcherby, indignant at the idea of being afraid of Angus, or that she cared for what he liked or disliked. "He ain't my master, and ain't going to put his foot upon me, I can tell him. He is my inferior in this house I would have you to know, and placed under me by master's orders ; and if he ain't, why I'll walk out of it, and let him do as he likes, which he shan't do while I am here, I can tell him."

" Shall I go and ask him if you may let mistress's sister in ? or do you think that he would be angry if you asked her to stop without consulting him ? It won't do to offend him, mother, will it ? for he has a deal of power here, and rules the house as if it were his own."

" You go if you dare," cried Mrs. Botcherby, thoroughly taken in, and out of patience at the thought of having to ask permission to do anything of Angus. " You go if you dare, and it will be the worse for both of you, for I'll lock up the house, and let me catch him trying to prevent me, that's all. I shall do as I like ; and so walk in if you please, Miss, and excuse my keeping you waiting so long, which ain't my fault, but all because of master's orders left to be sure and not admit people who came to ask for him while he was away."

The end was answered. Mrs. Botcherby had been admirably fooled, and the old woman clearly outwitted by the young ones. Angus had done the business. He had unconsciously assisted in a breach of his master's orders, and smoothed the way to what Miss Bertha proposed to do if she only had the opportunity, and could avail herself of Jane's assistance in carrying out her design.

" Mind how you go downstairs, Miss," said the housekeeper, staying to lock and bolt the door. " The house ain't very cheerful, I confess, just now, but then master and mistress are away, you know, and the servants on board wages in the town, and only Jane and myself to take care of the place. There's that wretched Angus, to be sure. But he's nobody, Miss ; a mere watch-dog, I may say, left to look after trespassers, and march up and down the outside room."

" Room ! what room ?" asked Bertha, suddenly alive to what she had been told of the constant guard Angus kept upon her sister.

" Oh, it's no room in particular, Miss ; so if you please just walk into the kitchen, and be so good as to excuse my asking you in there, for there's no fire anywhere else, in consequence of the house being shut up."

" The kitchen !" cried Jane, " why, mother what are you thinking of ? Ask mistress's sister into the kitchen, when I could easily light a fire in one of the upstairs rooms, and make all warm and comfortable by the time you get supper ready ?"

"As to supper," said Mrs. Botcherby, after a
pause, and slightly disconcerted at her daughter's
impudence, though she could not see how she
could oppose her in it, "there's not much choice.
There's a fine ham and plenty of new-laid eggs,
but then, you see——"

"The very thing. There's nothing like ham
and eggs·when you are in the country, or a fowl,
or something of that sort. You only get it ready,
and I'll sit here and warm myself, while your
daughter makes a fire and gets the bedroom
aired."

"Yes, that's all very well"—the old housekeeper began hesitating again, and looked at
Jane, as much as to tell her not to be so offi-
cious in making offers without first consulting
her—"but then, you see, as I said before, the
house is shut up, and——"

"We know all about that, mother, but as the
lady has kindly consented to excuse us and take
things in the rough, we had better say no more
about it. There's nothing more easy. You cook
the supper, and I'll light the fire in mistress's
bedroom, where you know the poor thing used to
sleep before the dreadful——"

"Why don't you go, then, and not stand talking there?" said Mrs. Botcherby, growing more
and more alarmed lest her daughter should say

what she ought not, or let the lady know more than was convenient respecting her sister.

Jane did not wait to be told twice, but taking a bundle of faggots and a light, she half turned her head to exchange looks with Bertha, then went upstairs to make a fire and get the room in order, while her mother stayed below to cook the supper.

Mrs. Botcherby was evidently ill at ease. She set about her task readily enough, but with a scowl upon her face, and a restlessness in her manner that did not escape Bertha's notice. She therefore thought that it might be as well if she tried to ingratiate herself in the old woman's favour, and made an attempt to assist, which was not however taken in good part, but put the old woman out, and made her more cross than ever.

Wishing her clearly to understand upon what terms she stayed, Mrs. Botcherby said to her—-

"Well, Miss, it is settled you are to stop here to-night, but not over to-night ; I shall get into trouble as it is if I am found out, and can only let you remain on one condition, which is, that you go away early in the morning, and never say a word to anyone of my having let you into the house while master was away."

"Not I. Besides, I have no one to tell it to, and you may take my word that I shall not mention it to Mr. Ellerton, which is not likely, as he may remain abroad some time, you know. Besides, I have no particular fancy to his knowing that I have been indebted to him for a night's lodging, for between you and me, we are not the best friends in the world, though I have tried not to show my dislike, as, of course, I do not wish to make my sister uncomfortable."

"Ah! well," said Mrs. Botcherby, "men are strange creatures at the best of times, and the Ellertons stranger than most. His father was the same before him, and I suppose he has his odd ways from him, and ain't so much to be blamed as some people think."

"And was his father of the same distrustful nature? Was he revengeful, and did he make himself a slave to his passions, or live the same unsociable life as his son?"

"Well, I can't say, Miss. But he was an Ellerton, and as far as I have seen, there's not much to choose between them. He had his troubles and his cares, poor man; but he bore them like a gentleman, and always conducted himself as such."

"He was kind to his wife at all events?"

"Oh yes, yes, kind as could be. But then you see, she died soon after they were married. That is, his second wife. She was master's mother, but the first I never saw."

" It is a comfort at all events to know that he had no example for his ill-treatment and suspicion. His father appears to have acted differently, and would have been ashamed to abuse a trust reposed in him by a gentle and confiding girl, after she had sacrificed herself for him, and given up the early hopes of life for his sake."

Bertha had said too much. She had touched on dangerous ground, and by foolishly informing the housekeeper that she knew of Ellerton's behaviour to her sister, set the old woman thinking that she had made a mistake, or been imposed upon; and that the best thing she could do would be to get rid of her, before mischief came of admitting her into the house.

Observing the old woman look at her and eye her sharply, Bertha took no notice, but thought to remove the bad impression she had made, by saying—

" You see, you dear, good old soul, there was another lover in the case; and you know when there has once been a first lover, the second has no chance, even if he is perfect as an angel. I have not the slightest doubt that Mr. Ellerton has proved a most excellent husband, and done all he could do to make my sister happy. But what of that? If she has still her old lover in her mind, he may break his heart trying to please her, and not

succeed ; so that I think he has done the wisest
thing in taking her abroad, where she will have
time to forget all about him."

This seemed to quiet Mrs. Botcherby a little,
though it did not remove her suspicions. She
made no reply, attended to her cooking, but
every now and then turned sharply round as if
with the expectation of catching her visitor betraying herself, or saying something that she
could lay hold of.

But Bertha was on her guard, and said nothing
more till Jane returned, when thinking to put
the old woman in good humour she pretended to
be very hungry, and said that she should like to
eat her supper in the kitchen, but looked at Jane to
let her know that she meant exactly the reverse
of what she said.

There was no occasion for Jane to interfere.
Mrs. Botcherby had already settled that the supper must be carried upstairs, as Angus might
come in and find the lady in the kitchen in defiance of his master's orders. She was not exactly
afraid of him, but she did not wish to quarrel
with him, since she knew the hold he had upon
his master, and that if he once took it into his
head to oppose her, she must submit, and leave
him master of the field, which she did not want
to do.

All things being ready, Mrs. Botcherby bade her unwelcome visitor good-night; said she hoped she would enjoy her supper, and told her not to be frightened if she heard anything in the night, such as cries and shrieks, which she informed her were sometimes heard, but not always—for she was subject to fits and did not know what she did, though she was told that she cried and shrieked, and therefore prepared her beforehand not to be alarmed if she called out, which she hoped she should not, and disturb her rest.

Suppressing a shudder, and knowing that the old woman intended to prepare her—not for her own, but for her sister's shrieks to come upon her in the dead of night—she promised not to be afraid, but to put the noises down to the right cause, and sleep all the better afterwards.

"Good-night, you dear old soul; please call me early, and then you know I shall have time to take a walk about the grounds before break-fast. After that you must be so kind as to let your daughter show me the way into the town, where I can take the coach and return home; disappointed, I must own, at not seeing my sister, but much obliged by your attention to me."

Following Jane upstairs, Bertha found a good

fire in the bedroom and the supper ready. But she had no appetite. The mention of those midnight cries, the evident suspicion the old housekeeper had of her, and the sight of the room formerly occupied by her sister — completely unnerved her, and she was glad to sit and question Jane about her mother, and ask if she thought, from what she had said, that she was likely to suspect her motive in coming, and would try to prevent her carrying it out.

Jane shook her head when she heard the conversation that had taken place below stairs repeated, and did not seem quite so easy as she had been at the presumed state of ignorance in which she had hoped to keep her mother. She knew her devotion to her master, her constant desire to serve him and obey his instructions to the letter. She also knew the difficulty they had had in inducing her to consent to let her in, and began to be seriously alarmed for the success of their scheme, should her mother discover the least inkling of Bertha's motive in coming to the house.

But, as it would not do to be afraid, and as they had not only to deceive her mother, but Angus—Jane advised that she should eat her supper as if nothing had happened, and not give her mother the least reason to suppose that she had assisted her in gaining admission to the house with a view to ultimate proceedings. The chief thing to do, was to persuade the old woman to go to bed, and then perhaps she might devise some means of coaxing Angus from his post, and leave the road clear for what they hoped to accomplish.

Whispering to one another, and talking of what they hoped to do, they were suddenly alarmed by hearing a creak upon the stair, and then a scuffling outside the door as if some one were listening.

Jane knew that it was her mother, and motioning to Bertha to eat and take no notice, she kept bustling about the room so as to prevent her mother supposing that they were aware she was outside—speaking in brief whispers, or purposely aloud, to let her hear what they said, which they took care should contain as little information as possible—until they had the satisfaction to hear the old woman go downstairs no wiser than she came, and slightly tottering in her steps.

Her mother got rid of, it became necessary to think of Angus. The curtains were drawn to prevent the fire being seen, and then Jane thought that though he would be sure to be on his watch close under the windows, that he could see nothing, and would remain unconscious of what was taking place within a dozen yards of him, if they only exercised a little caution.

Their further whispering was put a stop to by Mrs. Botcherby's cracked voice calling from the bottom of the staircase, and wishing to know how much longer Jane was going to be before coming to bed.   There was her gruel to be made, she said, her shoulder to be rubbed, and a dozen things to do, and yet she still kept chattering, leaving her to catch her death of cold at the foot of the stairs, where the draught was strong enough to turn a windmill.

Jane, like a dutiful daughter, said she was " coming ;" and as she had a personal interest in her mother's having a good night's rest, she offered to make her gruel for her, and put something in it that would do her good; something hot and strong; something good for rheumatics, and known to be unfailing in the most obstinate cases the most obstinate old woman ever suffered from.

" Coming, mother," cried Jane again, when she found that she would not go to bed without her, " coming ;" then, in a whisper, begged Bertha to make as little noise as possible and, above all, to be careful not to let Angus hear her or see the light. " Leave me to do the rest," she said. " I'll manage him ; or if I can't, I'll find some one who can. Good night, Miss ; keep a good heart, and by God's mercy all will come right."

Away went Jane with the supper tray, as a

good excuse for having waited, and met her mother at the top of the staircase; her patience by this time exhausted, and her temper on the rise, her rheumatism worse than ever; and Jane the cause of all, for not coming sooner.

Bertha heard the altercation; then, listening till all was still, she closed the door, and moving on tiptoe across the room, began to make a silent inspection of poor Margaret's bedchamber.

CHAPTER XI.

THANKS to Jane's care of her, there was a good fire in the grate, and a supply of fuel to last through the night. The candles had not been lighted; but as the room was light enough without them, Bertha very properly let them be, lest they should attract the watchful eyes of Angus, whom she heard pacing up and down under the window, and humming the burden of some wild song.

This, then, was her sister's bedroom! the room in which she had so often sat to watch the sun set and the glimmering stars, brooding over her forlorn condition, the misery of the future, and the blighted past.

Searching about in hopes to discover some memorial, or some record, of her poor sister, she saw two closets full of dresses and sundry articles of general wear. There was a wardrobe too, a large and handsome piece of furniture, in which she expected to find more dresses, letters perhaps, or memoranda, containing a brief recapitulation of her daily life.

It was locked! and, forced to be contented with the little she had seen, she gave up all hope of discovering further traces of her sister, when she observed a door left partly open, communicating, as she supposed, with a dressing-room.

The door was open, and as no great harm could come of peeping, she looked into the room, but saw little worth notice beyond a few boxes, a piece or two of old furniture, sundry articles not in daily use, and odds and ends of various sorts.

Beyond that room, lighted by the moonlight glimmering through the window, she saw another chamber, separated from the first by an archway built across, but so arranged, that it appeared to have been contrived with a view to throw the two rooms into one, and increase the size of both.

As there was no key to the door, she was forced to leave it as she found it, ajar, though she would gladly have locked it; for there was something in the appearance of those rooms that struck her with an uncomfortable feeling when she reflected, that she had no means of separating herself from them by any means she could perceive.

There was a second side-door to the bed-chamber, corresponding with the one she had just opened, and this, she imagined, led to Mr. Ellerton's dressing-room; but that door was locked,

and as it was of no use sitting up, she prepared
to go to bed, as Jane had promised to be with
her early in the morning· to arrange about a
meeting with her sister, if she could only manage
to͵ get Angus away, and leave her at liberty to
do as she proposed.

Resolving not to be nervous, and to forget
those desolate shut-up rooms, she sat over the
fire before getting into bed, and falling into a
reverie, began to think of her sister, as she had
seen her last, in all her pride of youth and beauty ;
and painfully contrasting her present misery with
her former happiness, reflected on her image till
her eyes filled with tears, and she was determined
to risk everything to get to see her once again, or
at the least to talk to her, and hear the sound of
her dear loved voice, in spite of all impediments.

She knew the difficulties she had to encounter,
and that courage was necessary in facing them.
It was of no use sighing ; she must act, not weep,
and give over reflecting, if she wished materially
to assist her sister and set her free from the
barbarous usage to which she had been subjected.
All she had to do was to exercise care and caution,
and in a little time Mr. Ellerton might find himself in a position he little expected, if she could
only set her sister at liberty before he had the
chance of carrying her away beyond their reach.

Was that Jane upon the stair, or had she fallen into a doze and slept longer than she thought? No; the creaking noise was plain enough—some one was moving outside the door! She heard it more distinctly now; and starting up in alarm, not knowing what to expect, heard the key turn in the lock and the bolt shoot home.

She had been fastened in the room! with what object she could not imagine; and terribly frightened, though at the same time determined to be satisfied, she tried the handle, but found her fears confirmed, and that the door had been locked on the outside to prevent her getting out, or anyone coming to her.

Could it be the housekeeper? or, had Angus discovered her, and imprisoned her to keep her safe? She could not stir! She could not even help herself now, much less her sister, and all her hopes of setting her at liberty appeared defeated—unless Jane could contrive to open the door, and communicate with her unknown to the person or persons who, evidently suspecting her, had fastened her in, to hinder her doing anything they disliked.

She did not dare to stir—hardly to breathe—for fear of making a noise. Her policy was to remain perfectly quiet, and not appear to be

aware of what had taken place, and so take off
suspicion from her movements. But to be shut
up there, to be detained a prisoner, or only have
the door opened when it was too late, and after
Mr. Ellerton had perhaps returned to find her,
and make her sister suffer still more severely
because of her attempt to rescue her, almost
drove her wild. She could have screamed,
knocked at the door, and beaten it to pieces, but
dared not, and felt that nothing was left for it
but patience, and the most miserable despair that
ever fell to the lot of an unhappy woman to
endure.

Angus was on the watch. She heard him
pacing up and down, ready to do anything his
master told him, or what would make him safe.
Murder had no terror in his eyes—death no
horror. Brutal, and wild, and rough, who knew
what he might do if she attempted to escape,
or cried out in alarm, and begged of some one to
come and set her free.

As to reflecting calmly on her situation, she
could not. She had enough to do to avoid
screaming ; but as she was sensible that the least
expression of alarm would tell against her, and lead
them to expect that they could frighten her into
submission, she determined to keep quiet, though
she could not shake off the dread she felt of what

she might have to endure at that wretch's hands, should he discover her attempt to outwit them.

But her sister, what had become of her? Expecting, yet fearing to hear the cries and shrieks the old woman told her to be prepared for, she sat and listened until she fancied that she heard her call, not in wild screams, but in low, sad murmurs and a voice choked with sobs. It might be fancy—it might be foolish and absurd to think so, but think it she did, until her sense of hearing became so sensitive, each noise, each whisper of the night, grew magnified into terrible distinctness, and the very rustling of the leaves assumed the accents of the human voice.

But to sit there all the night a slave to terror, unnerved, when she required all her firmness, and might have to make use of her energies at a minute's warning, would never do; so, partially undressing, she got into bed, and, covering her head with the bedclothes, tried to sleep.

It was impossible—at least she thought so; but by degrees, she grew less nervous, and as nothing occurred to startle her, she fell into a doze, woke up, dozed again, and then went fast asleep.

She woke up with a start! Something had disturbed her, or touched her, and pulled the bedclothes! She was certain of it; for she was

dreaming at the time, and should not have woke
unless she had been roused by something.

Yes, there it was again ! There was no doubt
this time; she felt it plainly—a gentle pulling
at the coverlid; and though she held it tightly,
it was drawn and pulled, while a low, soft voice,
singing .close beside her, murmured indistinctly
in her ear.

Fearing she knew not what, and waked up so
suddenly by that unexpected touch, she resolved
to know the cause of her alarm, and throwing the
bedclothes off, she saw, between the fire and herself, a figure crouched upon the foot of the bed,
and dragging at the coverlid with both hands.

The fire was bright, though low, and enabled
her to detect that the figure was that of a woman,
but so wild in her appearance she almost trembled
to look at her. It was not Jane ! Yet who else
could it be, unless some one had got into the
room thinking to frighten her.

It could not surely be Margaret ? It was !
She saw her face distinctly now. Though worn
and wasted to a shadow, she knew her, and leaping
out of bed folded her in her arms; then, in an
agony of tears, wept while she talked to her, and
endeavoured to make her understand that some
one was near who loved her dearly.

It was useless ! for though she suffered herself

to be embraced and folded to her breast, she
gave no sign of recognition beyond a faint sad
smile, and a gentle pressure of the hand, as if to
let her know that she was sensible of her kindness,
and aware that she was not one of her usual jailers.

There did not seem to be a possibility of
rousing her beyond this point.   She said nothing,
and did not seem to understand, when asked, how
she came there, but shook her head, and did not
appear capable of the least mental effort, or of
comprehending what Bertha in her anxiety said,
hoping to make herself known to her.

Oh, what a change !   Those sallow cheeks
and hollow eyes told her sad fate too plainly.
Her hair was matted and hung about her head in
wild disorder, while her poor hands clasped within
her own, had grown so thin that they more resembled a child's hands than a woman's, and were
as cold as ice.   She was so miserably clothed, too,
it struck her to the heart to see her in such a
wretched state, and snatching off a portion of her
own garments, she threw them over her, and
drawing her towards the fire, knelt at her feet
and endeavoured to rouse her from her lethargy
by chafing her limbs and talking fondly to her.

Time was precious, and though she would have
gladly sat and talked to her half the night, she
knew the necessity for immediate action too well

to neglect the opportunity her sister's unexpected presence afforded of assisting her to escape.   She had first of all to find out how she came there ; to lead her back the way she had come ; and should it prove, as she hoped, a secure retreat, to avail herself of it, and make the attempt immediately.

But the door! She had heard it locked. The side room door was locked as well, and unless Margaret had been concealed in the further of the two rooms at the time she looked into it, she could not imagine how she had got into the bed-room, or by what means she had eluded the vigilance of her keepers ; one of whom she knew to be on the watch, and tramping up and down to prevent the possibility of her escape.

It was running a great risk, but as it was important to ascertain how Margaret had found her way into the bedroom, she lit a candle, and going into the shut-up chambers, examined them closely, but could discover nothing in addition to what she had already seen, except the old-fashioned wainscot, the large bay-window, and the moth-eaten curtains, which fortunately for her prevented the light shining through them.

She had completed her investigation, and was about returning to join her sister, when, on turning, she saw her at her side, and starting in amazement, could scarcely believe that she could have followed her so softly ; she had neither seen nor heard her creep out after her when she left the room, though she evidently must have done so soon after she had quitted it.

Half frightened, and at the same time anxious to soothe, and not alarm her by any show of violence, she took her gently by the hand and endeavoured to lead her back; but Margaret would not suffer her, and breaking from her grasp, she ran towards a corner of the room, and kneeling, began to remove a portion of the wainscot, and revealed an aperture of sufficient width and breadth for her to pass through on her hands and knees.

Without giving her time get away, Bertha flew to her, and begging and entreating of her to remain, she so far prevailed upon her that, though she seemed fully aware of the necessity of returning to her prison before her absence could be discovered, she appeared to understand, and in a half-unconscious state permitted her sister to hold her back, and coax her by words and signs to do as she desired.

It was plain enough now. The secret of her passage into the room was easily explained, and though the woodwork effectually concealed the hollow space behind it when in its place, it was visible enough now that the skirting was drawn

back, though on her first passing through it, her
sister had had cunning enough to mask the
opening by placing the board in its original position to prevent it being seen.

By what means her sister had discovered that
passage leading from her prison to the interior of
the house, she could not ascertain ; whether immediately preceding her appearance in the bedroom, or if she had frequently resorted to it. She
only knew that she had found her way by it now,
and thanking her good fortune that she had
her when she least expected it, hoped to set
her at liberty more readily than she had
anticipated.

But as they passed the old bay-window, and
before Bertha had time to prevent her, she
sprang on one side, and uttering a stifled scream,
threw herself upon the ground, then with a
frenzied look, began tearing at it with her hands,
and moaning piteously.

Terrified by the wildness of her manner, and
afraid that Angus might hear her and be aware of
her flight, Bertha first used entreaty, then force ;
and carrying her into the next room, resolved at
all hazard to regain her sister's liberty, and her
own, without loss of time.

The room door was fastened. That she knew.
But the other door, that leading to the dressing-

room, did not shut closely, for between the door-jamb and the door she observed a narrow space, and began to think that if she could only insert something of sufficient strength between the door and the frame, she might wrench it open.

But there was nothing, no instrument, and nothing sufficiently thin, yet of sufficient power, to act as a lever. What was she to do ? A small iron wedge, a rod, a bar, anything that could be obtained under ordinary circumstances, would save them, and yet she was unable even to make the trial for want of such an instrument.

There was a curtain-rod in a corner of the room, it was true, but that could never be forced into so narrow a space as that left vacant between the door and woodwork. But on taking it up and observing the flattened ends, she pressed one of them into the crevice, and found it bite, and the door yield, though not much, as she pulled the other end and pressed it back.

She tried again, and again the door yielded. Then using greater force, expected to see the door fly open. But the rod broke short off, and she was left as powerless as before.

Yet not quite so powerless, for the broken end stuck fast and formed a wedge. She could get a better purchase now, and on applying the other end of the rod, found, to her delight, that the door gave considerably. Another wrench and the lock yielded; a piece of splintered wood fell to the ground and the door flew open.

There was nothing now to prevent their making their escape if she could only keep up her own courage and support her sister at the same time. She was a weak and feeble girl, but she was desperate; and feeling that upon her courage her sister's preservation depended, she prepared to exert it, though she trembled all the while, and indeed seemed much the weaker of the two.

Leading her sister through the door, and feeling her way in the darkness, yet starting back at every second step, as she thought she saw some one creeping before them, or lying in wait to carry them back again, she found herself in the dressing-room belonging to Ellerton, and close upon the head of the staircase. Here she took better heart, and speaking softly but encouragingly to her sister, was glad to find that Margaret appeared to rouse herself, and instead of it being necessary to lead her, that her sister beckoned her to follow; but on reaching the hall door, stopped suddenly, as if not knowing what to do, now she had got so far.

The door was locked and barred: Mrs. Botcherby had taken good care of that after having let her in—and afraid of making the slightest noise in drawing the bolts, the poor girl trembled and shook, and could hardly summon strength to remove the fastenings. But when they were removed, and the door was thrown open, Margaret all at once appeared to be a different woman: she stood erect and firm, drew in her breath as if she knew that something was expected of her, and that it was her turn now to support her sister and take care of her.

Weak from her long confinement, and trembling from head to foot with the new feeling of excitement that had come upon her, Margaret led her sister on, and stimulated by the fresh night air, and the sight of scenes she had once been familiar with, she struck across the lawn, walked swiftly in the direction of the meadows, and beckoning her sister to follow, led her by ways best known to herself through a coppice into the fields.

They were close upon the stile now where she had seen Angus and the gipsy, while she had sat beside the pool and listened to their conversation. Afraid, as it would seem, of what she had then heard, or dreading to encounter Angus in his midnight rounds—she pressed forward hurriedly, and never paused till she had led her sister over the second stile into the road, and far away from the miserable room in which her husband had immured her.

Her recollection seemed to fail her here. Her strength gave way, and all at once, as if her mind were wandering back to its old state, she seemed to lose her recollection, and to pause, then looking wildly round, uttered incoherent cries, and appeared incapable of proceeding further.

CHAPTER XII.

LEFT to her own resources, and uncertain which way to turn, or where to go to avoid being seen should they be pursued, which she feared they should be the moment their escape was known, Bertha had to exert, not only her fortitude, but her strength. She had to conduct her sister to some place of shelter for the night, and nothing short of death should make her give up the attempt, or leave her to the mercy of her barbarous jailer if she could prevent it.

Her first thought on quitting the high road, was to creep into some lane or copse, where they would be less likely to be observed, and might, if the worst came to the worst, obtain a shelter in a barn or outhouse, and so secure a rough protection · from the night. Anything was better than leaving her sister exposed, not only to the chance of being discovered, but to the chilling influence of the damp night air, which appeared to distress her greatly, for she shivered and clung to her as if for warmth, and by so doing made her doubly anxious to obtain a shelter for her as soon as possible.

13—2

She had already wrapped what covering she could spare about her, and folding her in her arms, and speaking encouragingly to her, tried to laugh, hoping to rouse and help her on her way. But it was useless, and trembling when she thought of the danger that her sister would be exposed to should she break down as well and leave her to her own resources, she did her utmost to preserve her courage, although, poor girl! she had enough to do to support her sister and herself, and not give way to tears and lamentations.

And thus these two poor wanderers kept sadly on until they gained the entrance of a green lane, down which they turned, and where Bertha hoped to find some wayside hovel; or, better still, a farmhouse where she could house her sister for the night; for, greatly to her alarm, she began to exhibit signs of weakness, making her doubly anxious to procure the assistance of which she stood so much in need.

There was no time to be lost, unless she wished to see her die or fall into the clutches of the villanous wretches from whose barbarity she had rescued her. She could hardly crawl along; stumbled at every step, and though she did her best to help her on, she had to endure the bitter grief of seeing her first stagger, and then sink down upon a piece of sward in a half-fainting state.

To see her lie on the damp grass, and know that she had no power to help, was something terrible. She knew that she must die if left exposed to the cold night air, and aware that in her enfeebled state a sudden chill might prove fatal, she wept and cried, called, but received no answer, then falling on her knees begged of the Almighty to befriend her in her helplessness, and save her sister from the fate she apprehended.

Heaven sent that succour. Her prayer was heard, and rising from her knees she heard footsteps, and then the tones of a man's voice, either talking to himself, or arguing with a companion.

The footsteps drew nearer, and just at the point where the lane widened and the piece of sward spread out—she saw the man himself; saw him emerge into the light, and then began to tremble for her sister and herself, as she observed him stop and look towards them, then give a loud whistle, as if to some comrade, and dreaded his approach almost as much as she had wished for it.

The man did not seem to be in too great a hurry to advance, but looked as if uncertain what to do, and as if he had some difficulty in deciding whether to come on or go back. Margaret was lying on the ground and Bertha leaning over her; a sight enough to startle anyone, and make a man think twice before he ventured to draw near.

"Who's there?" he shouted. "Is it a boggle or a ghost—a dead woman or a live un, or some one that's got out of his grave an' wants me to put him back again. An' you no speak, an' quick too, deil tack me if I don't run away an' leave you to yoursens."

"For mercy's sake—for pity's sake!" said Bertha.

"Eigh! but it's a woman's voice for sartin— though whether she's alive or dead there's no knowing, sin' it's my belief that a woman's tongue will still be wagging, even a'ter the breath's out of her body."

"Oh, do not leave us," cried Bertha, seeing that the stranger still hung back and preserved a respectful distance. "My sister has fainted, and will certainly die unless I can obtain assistance. You will not, I am sure, refuse to help to carry her where she can be attended to when you see the state she is in."

"Eigh, but I'm not so sure of that, for a man must ha' a confidence in hissel not often to be met wi' to trust hissel with two women at aince. I'm no a leddy's man at the best o' times, an' just the noo I'm no inclined to try the experiment on being axed, do you see."

" If you have a man's heart, do not refuse us the assistance you can so well afford, and for which I promise to reward you, if you will only treat us kindly, and place us where we may obtain a shelter for the night."

" As to a reward, lass," replied the stranger, less gruffly than before, " it's what I ha' been expecting any day these twelve months, till I am well nigh ruinated wi' sleeping at inns, an' paying exorbitant prices for a bite an' a sup. Oh, they're a bad lot are them innkeepers, an' not a pin to choose between 'em, whether you go North or whether you go South."

" Don't talk in that strange way, for the case is urgent. Unless you assist us and at once, it will be too late ; my sister will die."

" Eigh, but she does look badly," said the Northumbrian, drawing closer, and looking at Margaret as she lay on the ground. " But what in the name of fortune does she lie there for, instead of getting up like a sensible woman—an' asking for a shake-down at some hoose or other ?"

" How can you talk in that ridiculous way," cried Bertha, losing patience. " Either assist us, or send us some one who will ; it is cruel to trifle with our distress."

" Weel, then, I'll just tell you what I'll do.
I'll e'en tack her up an' carry her where she can
get a bite an' a sup, an' a fire to warm her.
But you'll understand I'm no to be expected to
pay for it.   That's one thing; an' the next is,
that you'll promise to behave yourselves as
decent boddies, a' no tack advantage of a simple-
minded man, or I'll bundle her in a ditch, an'
leave you to get her out if you can."

" Anything.   Only carry my sister where we
can procure assistance, and I'll bless and thank
you for your kindness, and speak of you as the
best friend we ever had in the world."

" I want no acknowledgment.   I simply want
you to keep your distance a'ter I have lifted her
on my shoulder, so as to be sure you have no
bad design upon me, but are willing to conduct
yoursel properly, an' like a decent boddy.   There,
she's safe enough.   But, deary me, she's cold as
a stane an' light as a feather !   It's weel I came,
puir thing, or it's my belief she'd a died right
off, if she ain't half-dead already, an' perishing
like a wee bit child."

Rough in his manners, and selfish to the
backbone, the Northumbrian had somewhere
concealed about his heart a touch of pity, which
Margaret's appearance called into play.   He left
off complaining, told Bertha to make haste, and

not keep the poor creature waiting in the cold all night, but to run before, go down the right hand turning, and shout and call till some one came to help them.

Bertha did as she was bid, and running down a lane branching to the right, soon beheld the welcome gleam of firelight, a group of tents pitched on the sward, and gipsy women preparing their meal.

Bertha's tale was soon told. The women, who had stared on first seeing her, got up the moment they heard of her distress, and running into the lane, met Mr. Bostock, bearing what appeared to be a lifeless woman in his arms, and taking her in charge, they wrapped her in warm blankets, and carrying her into a tent, busied themselves in preparing for her more immediate wants.

As to Mr. Bostock, he had done his part. He had brought the sick woman on his shoulder, and having got rid of her, troubled himself no further about her; but pushing into the middle of a group of men squatting round the fire, he selected the warmest place, and without more ado made one among them.

The men made room for him, but drawing sulkily on one side, scowled on him in a manner that ought to have convinced him he was more free than welcome, and that his presence was

anything but agreeable. But Mr. Bostock did not
care for that. He felt that he had a right to the
best place, and had taken it. He also felt that
as he had taken one of the tribe into his pay,
the whole of them had placed itself under a lifelong
obligation to him, which nothing but a slavish
obedience could ever repay; that he had a right,
not only to the best seat, but the best food; and
what was more, meant to have them ; more particularly as he began to doubt the trustworthiness
of his agent, and to think that, though he had paid
him so exorbitantly, that he was cheating him,
and making a bargain for himself.

Beyond looking at him for a moment the men
took no further notice, though they exchanged
significant glances among themselves, and threatened in dumb show; but the Northumbrian
never saw those threatening gestures, nor the
savage looks directed towards himself, or he might
not have felt quite so easy, as he stretched his
legs before the fire and kicked the ashes out of
his way, but have taken to his heels and run off
before they could attack him, and do him a mischief for some wrong that they fancied he had
done them.

But where was his friend in the velveteen
coat? He had come on purpose to see him, and,
feeling annoyed at his absence, he expressed his

discontent, not only as to his not being there, but at the general want of cordiality exhibited towards him by his companions, in his usual uncouth manner.

" Weel, you're a nice set, you are," he said, after he had had a pull at his flask, and corked it up again. " Here have I come on purpose to see that chap as I paid handsomely to do me a small matter, which he signally failed in, an' noo I am come to ax what he has done for my money he an't at home—if I may say ' at home' in a place like this, that an't fit for a dog's kennel, sitting by a fire that bakes you on one side while you freeze on the other. It's my belief that he's skulking, instead of working, an' spending my brass before he's earnt it."

But as the men still looked and said nothing, he felt intensely disgusted at the expression of their faces, which, now that he could see them more plainly, struck him as being more sulky and ill-favoured than ever. The swarthy skin, low brows, and keen, though partly discoloured eyes, all stamped with the same character, partaking of the same type, and the same individuality, which, in his opinion, was of the worst possible description.

Mr. Bostock did not know what to do. Instead of answering, the men scowled at him the more savagely on being questioned, and with a look as much as to say that he had better hold his tongue and not make too free with them. But Mr. Bostock was determined to be free, and began to express his sentiments on their want of manners in treating him as they did, notwithstanding what he had done for them, which, as he said, ought at all times to ensure him a welcome to their fire, and a sup from their pot, whenever he required to stretch his legs, or to pick out the choicest morsels.

The men did not seem to see it, but skulking off, left him by the fire without a word; never so much as replied to him when he inquired after his bosom friend in the big boots, velveteen jacket, and loose knee breeches, until disgusted at his treatment, he tucked his skirts about him, took another pull at his flask, and suspecting that his friend was otherwise employed in picking oakum or stealing fowls, slept in hopes of waking early in the morning, and of finding a good meal ready for him to fall upon, and take his revenge out of that.

CHAPTER XIII.

VIRTUE ITS OWN REWARD.

MR. BOSTOCK was a sound sleeper; he seldom woke till he was called, and when he got up, he expected his breakfast. He not only expected, but got it as a rule, and left an impression on the joint he cut, or the loaf he sliced, not easily forgotten. But Mr. Bostock was not in luck this time, for on waking he found not only no breakfast, but no fire; no one to abuse and bully, and the gipsies departed, where he could not tell.

A few embers were burning at his feet; picked bones and remnants of a feast he had not shared in were scattered about; the pot had been emptied, the kettle drained, and not a scrap left but a few potato peelings, as if to remind him that a substantial meal had been prepared and eaten while he was snoring on the ground, and dreaming of the meal he had hoped to share in, but had not.

He was hungry, thirsty, savage! and, vowing to be revenged, he kicked the embers in all directions, buttoned up his coat, then pulling his cap over his eyes, went fuming through the lanes into the road, where he put up at a small public,

and made up for lost time by eating and drinking
everything before him ; grumbled at the charge,
swore he had been imposed upon, and quitting
the house, started off in search of Angus, whom
he expected to find at his old quarters by the
stile or somewhere in the neighbourhood.

Away went the Northumbrian, spluttering and
burring down the road, and threatening un-
heard-of vengeance on the gipsy thief for taking
his money and doing nothing for it. He had promised to see Angus and get at what he wanted,
first for two pounds, then for five, and lastly, on
the promise of ten, had undertaken to find out
all about him, and let Mr. Bostock know the
result.   He had done neither ; and, determined
not to be cheated, he had started off to the green
lanes to make inquiries, and found the encamp-
ment on the old spot, but, greatly to his disgust,
no signs of his friend in the velveteen coat that
he had come purposely to meet.

His present object was to find Angus and
ascertain if his rascally agent had been tamper-
ing with him, that same agent having always
· boasted that he could get at him easily, and do
anything he liked with him, which Mr. Bostock
could not do ; whose policy had been to keep
out of the way, and not be known in the matter
till all was ready, then make his terms and bind

the other over to pay him handsomely. But since the vagabond had played him a dog's trick and left him in the lurch, he made up his mind to take affairs in his own hand, and ascertain for himself how matters really stood.

He could not have chosen a worse time. The housekeeper was half out of her senses at hearing that Margaret had escaped. Jane was completely bewildered, and Angus in a state of terrible alarm for fear his master should kill him on discovering what had happened.

Mrs. Botcherby dared not confess that she had admitted a lady into the house, and Jane knew better than to say a word about it, though by what means she and her sister had got away exceeded her comprehension, until they saw the door forced open, and Angus had lit on the aperture behind the wainscot, which at some time or other his mistress must have discovered, together with the secret passage leading from the outside room to the interior of the house.

It was plain enough now that it had been laid bare, and plain enough to perceive where the board had been originally fixed in the room below, and how easily it could be removed by sliding it back, or fill up the gap when returned. But then it fitted so closely, and retained its place so firmly, it became a matter of surprise how it should ever

have been detected—unless by some one acquainted with the secret.

That the younger Ellerton had discovered the
passage was clear enough, and that, familiar with
the ways of the house, he had effected his escape
without leaving a trace behind.   His mistress had
been less careful to conceal the aperture, but by
leaving the board loose, let people see how she
had got away, though perhaps she would have
made all safe had she come back the same way,
and not gone off, after breaking out of the room
above, through the hall-door into the garden.

But to make all sure, and be able to show his
master how it could be done, Angus squeezed his
body through the hole, then groping along, he
found himself in a narrow passage built between
the walls of the old mansion, and keeping forward,
discovered the board slipped back which masked
the second aperture, and passing through it into
the bay-windowed room, found himself at liberty
to go where he pleased.

That way his mistress must have gone ; she had
got clear off, and what should he say to his master
when he came back and asked for her ? He would
kill him !   Declare he had betrayed him, and
vent his rage on him for not having looked after
her more closely, though he had looked closely
enough, Heaven knew! and night by night had kept

his watch outside the door, thinking all kinds of horrors, and fearing at every step that some ghastly vision would start out and terrify him into madness.

It was of no use thinking ; no use searching ! He had hunted everywhere !—the park, the grounds ; and made inquiries in all directions. She was gone ! Gone where he could not find her, and, wearied with his fruitless search, he was returning home at the very moment that Mr. Bostock had finished his breakfast, and began thinking where he should find him.

He was not at the stile ; nor as far as he could see, anywhere about, though he looked in all directions, and kept walking up and down in hopes to find him, until tired with waiting, and thinking that he might meet him further on, he struck across the meadows, and drawing near the house, stood to pause and wonder at the dreary aspect of the place, and the rack and ruin everywhere exhibited. The grounds were in disorder, the flower stalks left to run to seed, the grass so long and rank, and the grounds so wofully neglected, that he began to calculate the cost of putting it in order, and feared that the remuneration he reckoned on would be considerably reduced if he did not at once assert his authority and turn out the present owner without loss of time.

Having determined what to do, Mr. Bostock
lost no time in putting it in execution.   Leaving the pleasure-grounds and the grass-grown
walks to take care of themselves, he walked
towards the house, then forward to the Avenue,
where he remained for a moment looking into
it, before he started off at a smart pace, tramping
through the long grass and giant docks, through
thorns and briars, until he saw, as he supposed,
the object of his search, sitting on the log of a
tree some distance off.

He had a capital opportunity of observing
him without being seen, for his head was resting
on his hands, and his hands leaning on a staff, or
something like it, as if he were in a brown study.
Still, he did not like the look of him ; and as
he had heard of his moroseness and ill temper,
he feared he might fly out in a passion at being
questioned—as Mr. Bostock wished to question
him—or, by taking the upper hand, keep him
under his thumb if he possibly could.

The place was so dreary, so far away from
help, so shut out from the world by the triple
row of trees, and the wild growth of thorns and
briars, that even presuming that Mr. Bostock had
been a much braver man than he really was,
there was some excuse for his feeling a certain
degree of nervousness at the thought of trusting

himself alone with Angus in a spot where he knew he might call and call, and shriek and shriek, and no one hear if he cried his heart out. But, as it must be done, he thought that he would have a good look beforehand and take stock of Angus, as he said, before he ventured to speak to him.

As far as he could judge, he agreed with the description given of him, and as the gipsy had said that he was fond of sitting in the Avenue, Mr. Bostock felt satisfied he was right, and that the veritable Angus Macleod was before him ; but brooding over something not very agreeable, for he kept his eyes so intently fixed upon the ground, that he did not even hear him, nor lift up his head, until he was close at hand, and standing within a dozen yards of him.

But as soon as he saw him, and before the other well knew what he was about, he started up, and then, as if not quite knowing what to do, whether to fly at him and strike him down, or run away—he kept staring at him, until he thought that it might be some one who wanted his master, or had stolen into the grounds to take a peep at the house.

In either case, he was in no humour to parley, but shouting to the intruder as he stood at a respectful distance, he demanded his business, and

14—2

told him to be off if he didn't want his head broke, for his master's orders were to warn off all trespassers, and keep the house and grounds free of them.

"Oh, it's all right," replied the Northumbrian, "an' you'll say so too, if you only listen to what I have to say; an' be glad to mack my acquaintance."

"But I tell you I don't want anything to say to you, and don't mean to have, so you had better be off before you get into trouble—coming where you have no right, and contrary to orders."

"Weel, noo, that's what I ca' downright ungrateful, a'ter the trouble I've taken in coming fra' the North to seek you, first in Jamaica, an' then down here."

"What do you know about Jamaica, or me either, 1 should like to know," replied Angus, a little less surlily, and as if willing to listen to what the stranger had to say, after his mention of Jamaica and the North.

"Oh, bless ye, I know a' about ye from the time ye were a babby till I see ye the noo, and looking as black as a keelman at a bad saxpence on a Saturday night. Eh, but you were a smart lad aince—at least they said ye were—when your father left you to be brought up by the gipsies."

" The gipsies ! What thief of a norken told you that, I should like to know ?"

" Eh ! but you're wrang to be so savage, for it warn't a gipsy. It war your awn blessed mither told me, who, puir soul, will be glad enough to know that I ha' found ye a'ter the lapse of time sin' she got you a situation wi' the puir boddies, who afterwards sent you out to Jamaica, thinking to make a man of you, on finding that you would no wark at hame."

" Who told you that ?" cried Angus, more and more confounded at the mention of the events connected with his early life, and of which the Northumbrian' took good care to inform him to get him to listen to him, and trust in him, if need be. " You're mighty glib with your tongue, and since you know so much, perhaps you know what happened to me after I left Jamaica to come back to England ?"

" Sure and certain. You were wracked, an' picked out o' the sea like a dead herrin' at the end of a line, that a person o' the name o' Ellerton threw to you an' pulled ye out. Though it's my belief, he'd no been so handy if he knew as much as I know, but would ha' pitched you back again, an' not ha' saved you to come down upon him some day wi' a claim he little dreams of."

More and more bewildered, and convinced that he knew everything connected with his past and present life, Angus beckoned to the Northumbrian to draw closer, then motioning him to sit beside him on the log, he appeared a little more yielding, though he could not help regarding him with a certain degree of suspicion, notwithstanding his professions of friendship towards him.

"I told you at the first," said Angus, "there warn't no trespassers allowed, but since you appear to know a few things about me, and may have a something to say, why let us sit down and have a talk. Not that I am much in a humour for talking, for something has taken place during the night that has put me out a good deal, I can tell you."

Invited to sit down, and finding that Angus was curious to know the reason of his seeking him, Mr. Bostock took it leisurely, seated himself comfortably, then pulled out his pipe and a small screw of tobacco, and after filling, handed what remained to Angus.

"It's not every day," said the Northumbrian, as he watched Angus press the remains of the tobacco into his pipe, and then light it, "you'll get a bit o' stuff like that; I bought it at Newcas'le, an' Newcas'le's about as famous for tobacco, almost, as Paisley is for bonnets."

Angus nodded, as much as to say "it's all right;" but as he did not seem inclined to talk more than he could help, Mr. Bostock was rather put out, though he made a virtue of necessity, and pretended not to notice it.

"I remember aince upon a time," he continued, cautiously approaching his subject, and wishing to ascertain if his vagabond agent had played him false, "I smoked a pipe wi' a gipsy chap I met out in the fields yonder, an' that war gude tobacco. Oh, he war a canny chiel that, an' wore a coat wi' big buttons, an' big pockets, that looked for all the world as if he had stolen it from a gamekeeper, or from some one as war half a dozen sizes bigger than himsel."

Angus looked up at this, and fixing his eye on his companion, drew comparisons in his mind between the coat he had seen the gipsy wear and the one described by the Northumbrian.

"He war a black-muzzled feller, of between your height an' mine, wi' a flat cap on his hed, an' lace-up boots on his big sprawling feet as war a mile too big for him. Eh, but he war an out an' out vagabond as ever you saw, an' a thief sin' the hour he war born I'll be bound."

"I know him," cried Angus, with an oath, "and watched him for a month or more, hoping to lay my hands on him, only he thought better of it, and never gave me a chance. It was a good job he didn't, or I'd have given him a crack with this, as would have spoiled him for thieving for some time to come, I can tell you."

" An' an awkward thing it would be to get a crack from," said Mr. Bostock, looking at the bill-hook, and glad to find that Angus and the gipsy were not the friends he expected, yet savage at being choused out of his money on hearing Angus speak against him in proof of their not being so intimate as the other had boasted. "Weel, then, we'll just wish he had had a crack wi' it, an' let him gang to the deil if he likes, where he'll be sure to find a hearty welcome, an' no one to find fault wi' what is done to him."

Angus saw no objection, but nodded as before ; and as they appeared to agree in their sentiments respecting the propriety of the place assigned to his treacherous companion, Mr. Bostock went on.

" It's no just that I wanted to talk wi' ye about, as you may suppose, or I should no a' come all the way from Alnwick on purpose to see you. It's a something of far more consequence, an' concerns you to know it, not only on account of your property, but for the sake of your sweet-heart—gin you have a sweetheart, as no doubt you have."

Angus brightened at the thought; Jane was

uppermost in his mind, and was standing before him in his fancy, dressed in her Sunday best, and looking prettier than ever. But he soon looked blank when he remembered that Jane had been the cause of the original mischief, and that to her meddling he was principally indebted for all the discomforts he had suffered. He was poor too; Jane was out of place; so that it was of no use thinking about her, though he preferred thinking of her to any one.

The Northumbrian had an eye like a hawk, and fixing it on Angus he knew for a certainty that there was a sweetheart in the case, but that there appeared to be some difficulty respecting her which it was his business to find out.

"Weel, then," said he, "it's no to be expected that a man can be blind to his awn interest, or so daft as to neglect it when he has a chance of pushing it. Now, I should like to know the man who wad be such a fool as to lose his sweetheart, when he could mack sure of her, or see her snapped up by some one else because he neglected his opportunity, an' did no marry her when he could, an' mack a leddy o' her without loss o' time."

"She's not a lady, nor's ever likely to be," replied Angus. "I'm not such a fool as that, or goose enough to look up to my betters. I know

my place too well for that, and so does Jane—
not that I mean to say she isn't a bit vain—
where's the pretty girl as is not, I should like to
know, who has a looking-glass before her and a
dozen or more fellows hanging about her, praising
her and telling her how smart and fine she is."

"An' why should she no be fine, or you look
up when you ha' a right, but don't at present
know how far; an' never would ha' guessed it
had I no taken the trouble to find ye out on
purpose to mack ye understand it."

Without in the least comprehending what the
other meant, Angus had yet a vague conception
stealing over him that his friend in the drab
great-coat had something to communicate to his
advantage. He had come perhaps from Jane to
say something kind, or to tell him that she had a
mind to marry him in spite of her snubbing and
her slights. Or his mother might have sent
him. His mother, of whom he had not heard a
word since he was a boy, and did not know that
she even lived until told so by the stranger.

"It's a lang story I have to tell you, but it
will keep. There's a deal to be said an' done
afore you will know the right o' it, which depends
on your paying me weel, an' treating your benefactor (meaning mysel) as he deserves."

"Paying!" said Angus. "I an't no money,

an' an't like to have. I am but a poor man, willing to serve master all the days of my life, and live upon his bounty like the faithful dog he says I am. Too faithful and too willing, perhaps, for the good of my soul! but I'll serve him for all that, and never grumble whether he pays me well or ill."

"Pay be hanged!" cried the Northumbrian. "It's you've to pay, not him. He is no better nor a cheat, an' can be proved to be such, spite of his swaggering an' his bounce. You only act wi' a proper spirit, an' reward me handsomely, he'll find it's a' dickey wi' him in no time, an' his fine estate slippit through his fingers as sure as my name's Dan."

"No ill words of master if you please, you sir, or I'll——"

"He ain't your master. The saddle's on the other horse; an' if you ain't a fool, you'll let him gang a'ter the gipsy, an' break stanes to earn a bit o' bread."

This was too much. Angus started up and might have done Mr. Bostock an injury, had not that prudent gentleman avoided the attack, and, by motioning him to resume his seat, convinced him of his anxiety to be good friends with him.

"You'll understand one thing," cried Angus, with slow and tolerably calm determination.

"The next time you say a word against master, over you go ; and I'll give you a lesson you wont forget by way of keeping your lying tongue between your teeth for the future."

"It's not a lee when I say you are a better man than you suppose ; an' it's not a lee when I say you may be married, an' tack your sweetheart to a better hame than you ever thought to tack her to.   But afore I tell you more for certain, I have a question to ax, an' I want an answer to it.   Now the question is, would ye—noo tack your time about it, an' no be in a hurry—would ye like to be rich, or would ye like to be poor ?"

"Rich, of course," cried Angus.

"I thought so.   It's only natural, an' what might be expected.   An' noo I'll ax you something else.   How would you like your sweetheart to be mistress of that hoose ?   How should you like to be maister of that hoose ? an' what would you gi' me if I proved you had a right to it, an' could establish your title to the satisfaction of the best la'yer in the land ?"

Angus took off his cap, and thrusting his fingers through his hair, appeared to be thoroughly bewildered : as he stared first at the Northumbrian, then in the direction of the house, where he could see the outside chamber and the abut-

ment of the old porch—then suddenly turned
pale, he shuddered, and casting his eyes upon the
ground, seemed as though he would dive into
the earth, and drag to light the secret evidence
of the crime he had committed.

The Northumbrian saw the action, but as he
did not know what it meant, he took no notice.
Satisfied with the impression he had made, and
knowing that he had but to strike the iron while it
was hot to excite the other's cupidity, and tempt
him with thoughts of his sweetheart in order to
make sure of his reward, he began to strike in
earnest.

"Noo you see, my friend," said Mr. Bostock,
"it was no lee I told you. You must be satisfied o' that, an' that I would no ha' put mysel to
the trouble, an' the cost of ferritin' you out unless I had a purpose in it. It's no Angus
Macleod you are at all. That's clear as two-
pence. It's not the name you were christened
by — though that says naething. You were
christened Arthur Craddock, after your father,
who war supposed to be a gipsy. But he
warn't! He war Arthur Ellerton! an' Arthur
Ellerton's son you are, which I'll prove to you,
as soon as ever we have made a bargain—the
maister of everything you see, an' the legal proprietor of what your uncle Mark has been keep-

ing warm, till he turns out into the cold to mack room for a better man than he can ever hope to be."

Half stunned, half stupefied, convinced, yet doubtful, Angus staggered to his feet; then sat down, and tried to steady his ideas; but not succeeding, he pulled out his pouch, filled his pipe, replaced the tobacco in his pocket, and began to smoke.

"If it would no be tacking a liberty, I'd just ax you for a pipeful in return for the one I gave you; an' though I don't expect such capital tobacco as mine war, I'll be content wi' what you have, an' no grumble because it ain't so gude."

Angus did as he was þid almost mechanically, then fell into a fit of thinking, from which the Northumbrian did not seem in a hurry to wake him, but filled his pipe and smoked for some time in silence.

"You see," said Mr. Bostock, retaining possession of the pouch in case he might want to fill his pipe again, "it's highly necessary we should come to a proper understanding an' arrange about the reward I am to receive for makin' your fortune. It's not a greedy man I am, understand that, nor an avaricious man; but brass is brass, an' as I have spent no end of

money in your service, it's only fair I should get
something to repay me for the long time I have
been absent from the bosom of my family."

Still Angus took no notice. He was too
much occupied with what he had heard to pay
attention to anything but his pipe; and as it
appeared to quiet him, Mr. Bostock thought the
opportunity a favourable one to settle the amount
he was to receive, before he enlightened him
further as to the true state of his affairs.

"You'll gi' me credit, I hope, for one thing,"
said he, "which is, that I am a gude-tempered
man, an' willin' to do a service to another if I
only see my way to making something out of it.
I am not a man of many words, but a fair dealing, plain-spoken man. Now you don't seem to
be a man of many words either, though it's your
mither's son you are, an' that makes it surprisin'!
Two bites at a cherry is a waste o' time when
one will do, an' so let's come to terms at aince;
when I will tell you what I have discovered, an'
mack all clear about your sweetheart, an' anything else you wish to know."

Angus opened his eyes at this. Jane was
deeper in his heart than he imagined, and as
the least reference to her excited him, Mr.
Bostock had wit enough to perceive it, and
sufficient cunning to take advantage of it.

" Weel then, we'll just say ten shillin' in the pund on all money you receive, an' five shillin' in the pund upon the vally of the estate, which we'll ha' a land surveyor to assess, at your expense, o' course. Will that do for you? Will you say yes to that? or nod your hed, sin' you'll no' tack your pipe out o' your mouth, though it's been out ever so long."

Waked up at last from thinking of what the Northumbrian had said about his being heir to the estate, of Jane being his wife, and of his master —his dearly loved master—to be turned out to make room for him, Angus did not appear to be too conscious of what he was about, and instead of replying, as Mr. Bostock expected, he held out his hand to take back the pouch, and looked rather angry when he found that he couldn't get it.

" Nae—nae—business first, an' pleasure a'ter, if you please. You only say 'yes,' an' as I'm an honest man, I'll send you from Newcas'le a pund o' the finest tobacco you ever smoked, though I pay for it mysel, just to show you what sort of a man I am, an' how liberal I can be when I'm treated fairly."

" Oh, hang it! 'yes,' " cried Angus; " though perhaps I shall alter my mind after all, and say to master——"

" Say what you like, but just say 'yes' again,

that's all, a'ter which we'll smoke a pipe together, an' get an agreement properly drawn by
some respectable la'yer in the town to mack it
binding."

"Why, 'yes,' then—damn it, yes—and don't
keep worrying with your yesses and your nods,
while I am almost mad, and feel more inclined
to knock your brains out, than pay you for what
you have told me. If it ain't a parcel of lies you
have been telling to make a fool of me, and put
thoughts into my head which oughtn't to be
there."

Catching his outstretched hand, and shaking
it heartily, the Northumbrian shouted " a bargain," and was about returning the pouch, when
he thought he might as well fill his pipe first,
and make sure of a bowl-full in case of accidents.

After taking as much as he wanted, he was in
the act of returning the pouch, when happening
to look at it, he turned it over in his hand, and
had a good stare at it ; looked at it again and
again, then at Angus, turned it inside out, and
searched in it with his fingers, as if he half expected to find something besides tobacco concealed
in the folding of the untanned piece of hide.

There was nothing. Nothing to repay his
curiosity ; and snapping the rusty clasp with his
finger and thumb, he said—

" If it's no taking too great a liberty wi' a
gentleman o' your property, may I ax how you
cam' by this pouch ?"

" Oh," said Angus, slightly confused, " I found
it."

" Again axing pardon for my boldness, but are
you sure an' certain you fund it, an' no had it
given you by the feller we were talking of just
the noo."

" I tell you no," cried Angus, snatching the
pouch, and thrusting it into his pocket.   " It's no
concern of yours how I came by it, so I'll thank
you to keep to what you've got to say, and be
quick about it, for I can't stop here all night."

" Nay but, Squire, it's a question I feel bound
to ax, an' must ax, sin' it's a matter of some
consequence to me, an' may be, is o' some consequence to you.   Now that bit o' hide, an' that
rusty hesp, I saw my ainsel in the hands o' a
vagabond as cracked o' what he could do, an'
how easy it would be to get you to do anything
he liked.   I'll tack my Bible oath o' it; an' that
makes me anxious to know how you cam' by it,
sin' fair dealing is what I go for, an' no taking
advantage of any man."

" Can't you be satisfied with what you're told,"
cried Angus, angrily, yet at the same time nervously, on finding the Northumbrian pressing him

rather more closely than he liked, as to how he came by the pouch, which he had kept as something handy, but secretly resolved to burn the moment he had a chance.

"I should be an unreasonable man not to be satisfied wi' what a gentleman like you tells me. But you see I ha' considerable interests to protect, an' as for aught I know this fellow may ha' been bamboozling me, an' selling my secret for less than the ten pund I promised him—I'll ax you to remember that you gave your word as a gentleman, an' said 'yes,' which you know is binding, an' better than a man's bond, only you see it an't so valuable quite wi' la'yers as a promise upon paper, wi' a stamp to it. But whar's the tooth, an' the child's caul? or did he swallow 'em, a villain, an' fund too late that he would no be saved fra' hanging, tho' he might fra' drowning?"

Angus was in a brown study; paying little attention to what the other said, he first dived his hands into his pockets with the air of a man not knowing what he was about, then taking them out, rubbed at the sleeve of his coat, and continued rubbing till Mr. Bostock interrupted him.

"Eh, but that's a smart looking button you've got there," said he. Then, with a look of infinite surprise—"As I am a man wi' a conscience,

I ha' seen that button afore too, an' on the very rascal's coat we were speaking of!"

In went the button after the pouch, and for a few moments the two men sat silent. The Northumbrian turning it over in his mind how Angus could have come by the pouch and button, and Angus busily reflecting if it might not be as well to knock the other on the head as he sat straddling his legs, and looking rather puzzled after what he had seen.

"Weel," said the Northumbrian, after a pause, "each man to his taste. You are for rubbing buttons, I for business, an' as it's time to set about it, I think we had better be off an' bind the bargain, when I'll put you in possession o' your property, an' tell you how to set about it to the satisfaction o' all parties. You've got the pouch, I own, but I've got the documents, an' the rascal who sold you that, or gave it you, could no cheat me there, or turn your master to the right about without first consulting me."

"Not so fast," said Angus, recalled to himself by the mention of his master. "It's not Angus Macleod as will show his gratitude like a cur, or bite the hand that feeds him; and though by walking up to that house I could go in and turn him out—take all, and leave him nothing—I'd sooner drop down at his feet and say, 'Take it, master, take all, do what you like with me, I'll go on as I have begun, and through thick and thin, show my gratitude and my love, for your having saved my life.'"

"Eigh? Weel, of a' the ungrateful scoundrels that ever lived, if you ain't the worst I'd like to know who is! What? would you ha' the rascality to cheat me a'ter I ha' made your fortune, an' ruinated mysel on your account? Oh, you're a slippy chap, a shally-walley feller, an' as timbersome o' doing yoursel a service as a mealy-mouthed lass o' saying 'yes,' a'maist. But I'll no be done, mind that. I'll bind you to your promise, or bring an action agin you, an' pop you into prison to pay costs, where you may lie like a rat in a trap, an' gnaw your way out if you can."

Angus had by this time risen to his feet. The Northumbrian had started up as well, and, in hopes of getting, if not money, yet revenge, might have had a tussle with him—when he saw a couple of men steal softly towards his companion, and in another moment catch him in their arms.

Angus fought and swore, struggled and raved, but as the men retained their hold, and told him "It was no use his struggling, as they had plenty of help at hand," he appeared pacified a little;

but on their attempting to handcuff him, he plunged and fought again, and had nearly broke loose, when a fresh couple of men ran from behind the trees to assist the others.

" What do you want with me?" cried Angus. " What have I done that I am to be pulled about in this way? which should be more than your lives were worth if I had my hands at liberty, and something in them to make you pay for it."

" You know well enough what you have done without my telling," replied one of the men; " but since you are so innocent, and want to know, why we have got a warrant against you."

" Against me?—what for?" cried Angus, trembling, and looking nervously about.

" Why, for murder, to be sure!"

" Murder!" shrieked Angus; "it's a lie, and you know it, and master knows it too, if you'll only wait till he comes back and ask him all about it."

As further struggling was useless, Angus gave over the attempt, though he still persisted in asserting his innocence, and begged and prayed of them to wait until his master returned, as he would be sure to speak in his favour, and not let him be carried off to prison to answer for a crime he had never committed; but as they paid no attention, proceeded to handcuff him, and told him that he had better go quietly, he was walking off between them, when he saw, to his horror, some of the men roll back the log of the tree on which he had been sitting, while others began digging, and turning up the earth over which it had been placed.

Mr. Bostock had been terribly put to it. Seeing his chance of making a fortune in danger of collapsing, he began to curse and swear at his ill-luck; while the people, who had by this time assembled, commenced making game of his burr and spluttering (which, now he was annoyed, had become worse than ever), and raised a shout at his expense every time he opened his mouth.

But what alarmed him most of all, was the presence of two or three of the gipsies whose coldness he had had so much reason to complain of the overnight—drawn, how he knew not, towards the spot where the men were digging, and who, seeing him there, began to talk and scowl at him so savagely, he was glad to get off while he could, and follow Angus towards the Town-hall, where, as he heard, the magistrates had already assembled to examine the prisoner on the charge stated in the warrant.

CHAPTER XIV.

THE COURT HOUSE.

THE report of a murder having been committed in the neighbourhood, and of the man suspected of the crime having been taken up, exceeded the best authenticated excitement recorded in the memory of man. There was no getting at the particulars, for no one seemed to know anything about them; but as it was confidently stated that a murder of more than ordinary atrocity had taken place, the townspeople felt called upon to stand up for the morality of their town, and hoot the accused person whether guilty or not.

Who had been murdered they did not know, but they knew the person accused, and as Angus had the misfortune to be unpopular, owing to the tales told of his sulky manner, and of his obeying his master so slavishly, the men were ready to believe him guilty without a trial, and the women to cry shame on him before they knew much more about him than the men.

The way up to the Town-hall was lined with people, some standing on doorsteps, some in the road, but all waiting to see the culprit pass. And when he came, when that pale-faced trembling wretch moved slowly by, handcuffed and guarded by the officers, all doubt (if any had previously existed) vanished. He was as clearly guilty by the way he hung down his head and staggered along, as ever man was guilty, and deserved to be hanged if only for his looks.

The ill name that Angus had acquired (little as he deserved it) was brought to bear against him in a way ill names generally are. There was nothing too bad for him, nothing too vile, and no crime he would not commit. Thus, while he scarcely dared to lift his eyes, dreading to meet some one he knew, or to see Jane standing in the road looking at him, the folks of the town made good use of their tongues, and spoke of him without the least regard to truth or reason ; abused him loud enough for him to hear, and declared that they hoped to see him hanged, and sent out of the world as soon as possible.

They were close to the Red Lion now, and facing it stood the all-important Court of Justice ; the unsightly old Town-hall built over the Market-place, resembling a first-floor on stilts, and looking directly into the High Street. The stalls were empty, market-day was not till to-morrow, and the few boys playing on the steps conducting from the Market-place to the hall o justice, had to be caned before they would make room for the beadle, and allow the prisoner room to pass.

Scarcely had he climbed those rickety uneven steps, when the London coach pulled up, and on alighting, one of the passengers, a tall dark man, who carried a cloak and a small valise, stopped to inquire what had happened, or if anything was the matter.

" I should rather think there was," replied a boy. " But they've got him fast enough, and there ain't no more chance for him than I have of getting in there," said he, pointing to the Court House.

" What has he been doing ?"

" An't you heard of the murder then, and who has done it ?"

" Murder !" The tall man repeated the word, and looked as if the very sound had had a strange effect on him.

" But he'll swing for it as sure as you stand there, so they say at least ; and I ain't going till I know."

Sensibly as the news appeared to stagger the tall man, he soon recovered himself, and was forcing his way through the crowd, when he heard his name mentioned, and observed that he ex- cited more interest among the persons surrounding him than he liked. But as he did not want to be stared at by a set of idle fellows, he was in the act of turning away, at the moment an old gentleman, hurrying along, met him face to face, and stopping short, bowed rather stiffly, as he said—

" Mr. Ellerton, I believe, and come I presume to speak to your servant's character. He will require a good one, I can tell you, to have any weight in rebutting the charge that has been made against him, and which I am informed can be brought home to him by a highly respectable and independent witness."

" What charge ? I am unacquainted with what you refer to, having this instant arrived from London, when I accidentally heard that a man had been arrested on suspicion of having committed an offence against the law."

" It is a terrible one. A crime of the greatest magnitude, but thank Heaven not of frequent occurrence in these parts, for I don't think there has been a murder in the neighbourhood for the last twenty years."

" Indeed !" said Ellerton, knowing how much depended on his calmness, and preserving it wonderfully. " But who has been taken up ? You mentioned his being a servant of mine ; I had several. Pray which one do you mean ?"

" His name is Angus Macleod. But we shall know more by-and-by, and if you please we will go into the Court and listen to the evidence. In the meantime, I may as well explain that the warrant was not issued until sufficient evidence had been adduced to justify the Bench in granting it, and I should advise you, Mr. Ellerton, as the son of my old friend and neighbour, to present yourself in Court, in order to avoid the possibility of any talk which might arise if you absented yourself on so important an occasion."

" If you think it necessary," said Ellerton, not wishing to go, yet not daring to refuse.

" I not only think it necessary, but in the highest degree essential." Then observing him still hang back. " But please yourself. You are the best judge of your own conduct, and of your man's character. All I can say is, that as a magistrate I shall discharge my duty irrespective of persons or position. I may also confidently assert, that my brother magistrates are quite as determined as myself to sift this horrible affair to the bottom, and to get at the truth of what strikes us all as involving contingencies of a most distressing nature. Good morning, sir."

Bowing rather more stiffly than before, and evidently not too well pleased with Ellerton's apparent disinclination to · present himself in

Court, the old gentleman walked up the steps into the Town-hall, and left him pale and anxious at hearing of the unexpected turn events had taken during his absence.

Angus had been accused of murder. He was in custody, and judging from what the magistrate said, he had reason to apprehend that he was not entirely free from suspicion of the crime himself. But who could dare to hint that, or breathe a word against him? It was not possible that they could associate him with his man's offence, or even name him in connexion with it, —provided it were the one he had urged him to commit, at his request, and to convince him of his gratitude.

No one knew of that. No one but Angus and himself; and unless he confessed (which was not likely) how was it possible that he could be implicated, or be suspected of a guilty knowledge of what had taken place? The particulars of young Arkwright's disappearance had yet to be discovered before they could act; yet strange to say, he had that very moment been, if not positively accused, yet broadly hinted at as sharing in his man's guilt, and heard his name associated with his servant's too plainly to question the old gentleman's meaning when he spoke of distressing contingencies involved in the offence, and of doing his duty irrespective of persons or positions.

He had no time for reflection, but in the space of a few moments must decide on the course to adopt; either to leave his enemies to take advantage of his absence, or confront them, and dare them to breathe a syllable against him. The proceedings would shortly commence, and one way or other he must decide at once. He chose the bolder of the two, and going up the steps, entered the Court House, where he saw Angus pale and trembling, awaiting the charge that would soon be preferred against him.

If he were so cowardly now, so downcast and so trembling, what would he be when the charge itself should be stated, and the evidence, if they had any, be brought against him? Had he but adhered to his original determination and got rid of him at the time he had it in his power to despatch him secretly, he felt that he should have been relieved of fear on his account, and free from the uncertainty he then endured—that at the least danger threatening his life Angus might turn round on him and say that he had set him on to commit the crime of which he was accused.

He had first to ascertain who made the charge; to learn the names of the witnesses, and then perhaps he might obtain some clue, and prepare for what he had to expect.

The Court House was so full that he had some difficulty in finding a place sufficiently removed from observation, yet near enough to the body of the hall, where, as he knew, the parties chiefly interested in the proceedings would be assembled, near to the magistrates, and opposite to the prisoner.

The first person he chanced to see, sitting with the air of an important personage, and whispering to a gentleman at his elbow, was the abominable little Captain ! He had no difficulty in recognising him, nor in ascertaining who were the accusers now. But if Angus only held his tongue and did not betray himself, he had nothing to fear, for they knew nothing, and could only allege suspicion at the most, against him. The gentleman to whom he was speaking was not, as he at first feared, the obtrusive clergyman, who had thrust himself into his house and spoken so largely of what he meant to do towards discovering his missing brother. He was quite satisfied of that, although at the first, and before he had looked at him attentively he had taken him to be the parson, and felt an unaccountable terror at his very sight. He was like him certainly, and yet so unlike, he wondered he could have been so blind as to start at seeing him, and not at once detect the difference between the upright, fearless bearing of the clergy man, and the affected dignity of the Captain's present friend.

His eyes too—those heavy, sleepy eyes—had none of the characteristics of the other; none of the lightning flash which sometimes, while he spoke, almost startled him into a belief that he had seen those eyes before, and longed for an opportunity to match them with the miniature, to see for himself how closely they resembled the eyes now closed in death, and no more to be gazed into with fondness by his faithless and inconstant wife.

Selecting a place in the body of the Court, he hoped to escape observation, when the Captain, wishing to stretch his legs and look about a little before business commenced, happening to look across, detected him at once, and, fixing him with his eagle eye, looked at him with ineffable disdain, muttered the word " coward," then, turning his back upon him, sat down in silent indignation.

This action, slight as it appeared to be, had the effect of attracting all eyes in the direction where Ellerton had taken his stand, and of drawing on him more attention than he desired.   But it was too late to alter it now, or indeed to stir without making matters worse; and silence being proclaimed, Angus Macleod was placed under examination on a charge of wilful murder, and the witnesses summoned to appear.

During the momentary pause that followed, and before the first witness got into the box, Angus lifted up his head and gazed about him in hopes that he might see some one in the Court he knew, who would say a word in his favour, or look compassionately on him. But seeing no one, and finding the eyes of the whole Court bent on him, staring at him as if he were some wild beast, he cast down his head again, then, hiding his face in his hands, appeared more timid and distressed than ever.

On the first witness being called, and after looking anxiously towards him, he appeared relieved on observing a gentleman step into the witness-box he had never seen before; or if he had, he did not recollect him.

The effect produced on Ellerton was of a different character. He started, then turned deadly pale. The Court seemed whirling round. His eyes grew dizzy, and he had to summon his utmost fortitude to appear calm at sight of the witness now standing in the box before him.

But when the witness answered to his name, the effect was still more startling, and for some time he appeared incapable of thought or action as he recognised in that witness the original of the miniature, then knew for certain that some fatal mistake had been committed, and that Angus, instead of killing the man he hated, had destroyed some one else.

It was Frederick Arkwright.

On being sworn, and called upon to give his evidence, Frederick (looking less like his brother now that he was differently dressed, and not at all like a clergyman) informed the Court that he had been engaged to Mrs. Ellerton before that lady's marriage, but in consequence of an unfortunate misunderstanding had lost her. Distracted at the intelligence of her fresh engagement, but unable to prevent her marriage with her present husband, he also stated, that as soon as he regained his health he followed her into the country, and, determined at all hazards to explain the cause of their unhappy separation, bribed a servant to admit him to the house unknown to her husband, and without the sanction of his wife.

Surprised and alarmed at seeing him, he found her, as he said, determined to remain true to her husband. Deaf to his entreaty, she resisted his efforts to persuade her to elope, and conducted herself through the trying ordeal not only as a loyal, but a true and constant wife.

" It is important I should explain this," he

said, " to relieve the lady from the consequences
of my imprudence, and clear her reputation from
any blame in this unfortunate affair. It is impossible to speak of her too highly, or praise her
more than she deserves.

"She was, as I have told you, surprised at
seeing me, and fearing her that husband might return, she endeavoured to persuade me to leave the
house. But I was obstinate and foolish, refused
to listen to her; and, deaf to her entreaty, was
about to plead to her again, when we heard her
husband ride towards the house, and in another
moment ascend the staircase, with the intention
of surprising us.

"Alarmed for my safety, and anxious to protect me from his fury—not that I dreaded it—
she led me to a flight of stairs, and telling me that
I should find a corridor at the bottom, leading to
the back of the house, she bade me go, and left
me.

"Obeying her instructions, though I confess
with reluctance, I succeeded in finding the
porch she had described, but on throwing the
door open, started back, as I saw a man dart
past, and run towards the shelter of a clump of
evergreens a short distance off. Judge of my
horror and alarm, when I saw a second man
emerge from the shadow cast by those very trees,

16—2

and as the other passed, strike him senseless to the ground! A second and a third blow followed, and before I could recover my alarm, or run out to his rescue, I observed the murderer standing over him with an uplifted axe, watching for the slightest sign of life or motion to make a fresh attack."

" Did not you endeavour to make some attempt to save him ?"

" I could not. The murderer was armed with a formidable weapon, I was defenceless ; and not wishing to risk an encounter which might have proved as fatal to me as to the poor unhappy wretch lying dead and bleeding on the ground, I remained sheltered in the doorway, and observing what passed, noticed the murderer go away after looking to satisfy himself that the man was dead, but afterwards return, and drag the body into an avenue lying a short distance from the house."

" What did he do then ?"

" Having dragged his victim to the centre of the grove, he began digging, and when he had dug deep enough, he threw the body into the grave he had prepared, then shovelled in the clay ; and rolling the trunk of a tree across, fell on his knees, and called on God to pardon him for what he had done to please his master, and to rid him of his enemy."

" What next ?"

" It then occurred to me—and after I had heard him speak of the murdered man as of some one his master wished him to kill—that *I* was the person meant to be despatched; that most probably my visit to the neighbourhood had been discovered, and that her husband, fearing I might endeavour to see his wife, had had me watched, and ordered his man to kill me if he saw me approach the house, or leave it while he was away."

" This is a serious charge."

" I know it, and am prepared to take the consequences. But from subsequent intelligence I am positive that it had been planned as I have stated, and that I owe my life to the presence of that man I started from watching near the house at the very moment I was passing out. Her husband returned home unexpectedly—he had received intelligence of my visit, and hoping to make his revenge secure, no doubt thought to take me in the toils, or drive me into the trap prepared for me, well knowing his man was lying in wait, and ready to execute his will upon me."

The impression made by this astounding revelation on the Court and auditors, was deep and general. It confirmed the belief already entertained that the accused had been suborned to commit the crime at another's instigation, and that however guilty he might be, he had been made the tool of his master, or of some person unknown.

Ellerton had heard himself openly accused of complicity in his man's offence; he had been associated with him in a deed of the blackest dye, yet did not dare to say a word, fearing Angus might be tempted to betray him in the hope to save himself. He saw his terror-stricken look, his intense anxiety, and the fearful glance he turned upon the witness as he recounted the particulars of what he had seen him do; staring at him in dread, and fancying that he saw the devil at his elbow ready to lay hold of him.

But when the news arrived of the body having been found, and the dead man's clothing was produced in Court, his terror knew no bounds. He shrieked and raved, and could with difficulty be quieted, when on matching the button found on him, it was seen to correspond with the others left on the coat, and as one was missing, there remained no doubt that it had been torn off in the struggle, or by dragging the body on the ground.

The pouch too. The very pouch Angus had wished to show his master, was recognised by one of the gipsies as belonging to old Daniel, but by what means it had come into his possession was

not so clear : though they began to suspect that
the scoundrel who had injured the old man had answered for his crime, and that Angus, by taking
it from him, had only added another link to the
chain of evidence, strong enough already, but
rendered doubly strong by this additional proof
of guilt.

Not wishing to say too much about it for fear
of compromising one of their tribe, the gipsies
hung back; but Mr. Bostock, taken completely
off his guard, and forgetting the damage he was
about to inflict on the long-lost heir, volunteered
his evidence, and on being sworn, said that he had
seen the pouch in the dead vagabond's hands a
dozen times, and knew it by its having a rusty
steel clasp, and an old woman's tooth in it.

Angus could bear no more : begging and im-
ploring for mercy, he stretched out his hands
towards the magistrates, and entreated that some
one might be sent to his master, who would soon
tell them the rights of it, for he knew all about
it and could get him off. Then, perceiving
by the looks directed towards where Ellerton
stood, that he was already present, he called
to him, begged of him, as he loved his soul,
to speak the truth, and not let him die for doing
what he had told him, though he had made a mistake and got rid of the wrong one after all.

" The fellow's mad," cried Ellerton, anxious
to put an end to the scene, and to avoid any
further appeal from Angus, or reiterated pro-
testations of his participation in his crime, " and
I must beg the Court to protect me from a charge
made by a ruffian, who would be glad to shift
the responsibility from himself, and inculpate
another, if he could only escape the consequences
of his crime."

" Mr. Ellerton," said the old gentleman who
had spoken to him outside the Court, and after
consulting with his brother magistrates, " this
is all very irregular, but under the circumstances
must be excused.   The case is open to suspicion,
we are bound to admit, but at the same time we
feel the force of what you say, that any
accusation made by an accused person against
another should be received with caution, and
not be taken as evidence unless backed by corro-
borative testimony.   That testimony is wanting ;
and though, as I said before, I and my brother
magistrates have considerable doubts in the case,
yet as it stands, you cannot be charged as an
accomplice on your servant's unsupported accusation.   Should, however, further evidence be
adduced, the Bench will be free to act, and however painful the task may be, we shall discharge
our duty to the best of our ability."

"I have to congratulate you, gentlemen, on your discretion; but as I do not wish to hear anything further of this wretch's outcries (although I came to speak what I know of his character, and that favourably), or of a witness's impertinent observations, I shall beg permission to retire, and save myself and you, a further proof of my servant's ingratitude to the man who saved his life."

"I know you did," shrieked Angus. "God bless you for it! But I can't die because of that! I can't, indeed, master, or I would: so speak the truth, and tell the gentlemen how I begged and prayed of you not to ask me, but you would, and persuaded me at last to kill him. Anything short of that I'll do; work for you, starve for you—but die! don't ask it, master, for it can't be done, though you may save my life a hundred times."

But Ellerton was gone! The Court adjourned, and Angus was committed for trial upon the capital offence.

"Weel," said Mr. Bostock, after the doors were closed upon him; "of a' the obstinate pigheaded chaps I ever saw, these Southerners are the worst. They'll no tack a hint, though you din it into their ears; nor see, though you try to open their eyes, an' all for nothing. It's my belief a' the 'cuteness an' the cunning comes fra' the North, an' all the talent too.   Eigh, but it's a bad world we live in, an' Dan Bostock no better than a fule to try an' mack it better."

His fit of morality and grumbling over, he began to think about refreshing his inner man, and as the evening was drawing to a close, where to find a bed at the cheapest possible rate.   The outskirts of the town appeared to be the most likely place, and keeping on the London road, he first eyed on one side then the other, hoping to discover the required accommodation.

The " Green Dragon " hung out its sign-board temptingly, but Mr. Bostock was not the man to try a night's lodging at an inn.   He wanted something cheap, something he could see his way to without much expense, and an honest simple-minded person who was willing to be content with what he chose to give.

But as he could not help casting his eye upon the larder, he saw a splendid piece of cold ribs of beef hanging just inside the door, and reckoning the cost of a good cut at it, he chanced to see the Captain and his friend at one of the windows looking out at him.   He had had enough of them already, that is of the younger one, for he had been the principal witness against his client, and the chief cause of all the mischief from first to last.

" Eigh, Mr. 'Green Dragon,'" said he ; " you'll
no do for me, nor the company you keep either.
The beef's gude enough, but the charge and the
presence o' that feller would mack it go agin me,
so I'll e'en walk on an' stand my chance of get-
tin' something at a cheaper rate, an' company
more to my mind.'

Swinging down the road and trudging on at a
tolerably good pace, he soon came in sight of the
lock-up, and pausing when he reflected that
Angus would most probably be confined there
until he could be conveyed to Maidstone Gaol,
he was seized with a fit of melancholy and, downcast at the change that had taken place, looked
anything but pleased.

He had not stayed there long when he heard
a buzz of voices, and in the distance saw the
constables and the unhappy prisoner coming down
the road, followed by a mob of people, hooting
and yelling, and shouting after him every oppro-
brious term that they could lay their tongues to.

Halting by the roadside, the Northumbrian
first cast a look of pity at Angus, and then
began silently to upbraid him for being such a
fool as to resort to vulgar crimes, when, if he had
only waited, he might have lived in style and
been a man of consequence ; not as now, a low
and brutal ruffian, hooted after, and mocked, and

laughed at every time he attempted to break
away, or get his wrists free of the handcuffs.

Looking from where he stood, he could see
the lock-up on one side, and the crowd advancing
on the other. They were close upon him now ;
the constables in front with Angus, the mob
surrounding them, or running on before, to get a
better sight of the prisoner, and wish that he
might be hanged without loss of time.

Poor wretch ! he looked half-dead already !
His face was pale, his eyes wandering and wild,
and he appeared so weak that the officers had to
drag him along, holding him up by the collar,
and pulling at him by his arms.

They were close upon him now ; so close, that
the Northumbrian thought the best thing he could
do would be to step on one side and let them
pass. But as he turned, Angus lifted up his
head and saw him ! Saw, as he thought, the
only friend he had in the world, and, calling to
him, begged of him to try and rescue him, or
go to his master, and see if he could prevail on
him to speak the truth.

The Northumbrian shook his head, and not
too well pleased at being recognised and called
to by an acknowledged culprit before so many
people, he stepped out of the road on to a
bank, but unfortunately slipped and fell, and,
on attempting to rise, fell a second time, having

trodden on the skirt of his long coat, and tumbled into the road.

The crowd had a new object now, and, making free with Mr. Bostock in a manner that he by no means relished, the people composing it kicked his bonnet first to one, then the other; tugged at his coat, and used him so roughly, that he lost temper, and began to lay about him so vigorously, he soon drew their attention from Angus to himself, though sorely against his will.

Seizing the opportunity, and making a sudden spring, Angus wrenched himself away; broke from the constables, and bounding over the fence skirting the road, was gone. The constables ran, but too late to overtake him, and as the fence was high, and the prisoner had got a good start, he appeared likely to keep it, and not give them a chance of taking him again.

The whole thing had been so sudden, and the escape so unlooked-for, that they hardly knew what to do. The constables stormed, the people shouted, and amidst the confusion the prisoner bid fair to get beyond their reach, when two rough-looking fellows, hanging on the skirts of the crowd, heard the shout, and, seeing what had happened, leaped the fence, and eager to revenge a comrade's death followed his flying footsteps, and, like a couple of bloodhounds let loose upon their prey, kept onward on his track.

CHAPTER XV.

THE impression made on the public mind—that is, that portion of the public mind represented in the neighbouring town—was dead against Ellerton. The appeal Angus had made, his frantic cries to him to speak the truth, and the earnestness of his declaration that he had set him on to kill some one he hated, were not lost upon his hearers, who began to wonder why the master had not been also taken into custody, and placed beside his man as an accomplice.

The news lost nothing by travelling, and, spreading in all directions, it was not long before it reached Mrs. Botcherby's ears, at a time she was in the greatest terror about her mistress, and had some thoughts of running away herself, and letting Angus bear the brunt of his master's anger. Just as she was hesitating what to do, she was startled by the news that Angus had been taken up on suspicion of murder, and, worse still, of the accusation he had made against her master, that he had set him on to commit it.

It might be her turn next, and like a prudent woman, Mrs. Botcherby determined to take her departure while she had a chance, and as Jane was there to help and pack up her bundles, they prepared to set off together, and leave the house to its fate, when unfortunately they met Mr. Ellerton coming through the lodge-gate, and in a terrible state of agitation at seeing them.

Then, for the first time, he heard of his wife's escape, and distracted by this fresh calamity, and incensed at the old woman's ingratitude for leaving him at such a moment, he went to satisfy himself how it had been accomplished, and by what unknown means. He would have rushed out then and there to hunt for her; ridden half over the county, and offered rewards for her recovery, but dared not, fearing to expose his own barbarity, and let it get known that he had imprisoned her, and shut her up to gratify his revenge.

He found upon inquiry the secret of her escape, and eager to satisfy his doubts, discovered the started board and the narrow passage leading from the outside room into the house. His brother had found that way before! The mystery of his disappearance was explained, but little thought of in the press of more important matters; of his wife's escape, and his own danger, should Angus's statement be believed, or corro-

borative evidence be produced to connect him
with the crime.

Could the old woman by any possibility fur-
nish that evidence? had she heard him rouse up
Angus on that night, and might she not be able
to supply the link between the two? Explain how
he had coaxed and tempted him, or, trusted by
Angus with what he had urged him to do, could
she turn round on him, and make his position
more dangerous than he had at first imagined?

She might! It was impossible to say. She
must have powerful reasons for quitting him so
suddenly, or be afraid that he might be tempted to
lay violent hands on her; or that she could be
made responsible for the share she had in keeping
his wife shut up, against the law, and in opposition to the dictates of pity and humanity.

What was he to do? Fly while he had yet
time, and leave the world to talk of him as it
pleased, while he should be beyond its reach and
safe from danger. It was madness to remain
where he was, or stay to be pointed at, and held
up to public execration as a man suspected of a
monstrous and inhuman act, or of having insti-
gated another to commit it. He had no two
ways to choose. He had but one; and that was,
to escape while he had the opportunity, and leave
the rest to chance; to bide his time, be rid of

Angus, and then, when all was over, return to be revenged on those who had so cruelly deceived and injured him.

It was night. He was alone. His servants had left him, and as to a friend, he had not one in the wide world who would speak a word of comfort to a now despairing man! He had his own thoughts, indeed; but they were doubtful and perplexed. He found no happiness in them, came on no refreshing spring, but traced an endless waste of useless and most vain regrets on every side; and reflecting on the little use that he had made of life, from childhood up to manhood, drew back—not to repent! not to regret! but resolved to do as he had begun, and obstinately maintain his own wrong-headed notion of what he thought was right.

His life was what he had to think of now, and how to preserve it, so as to enable him to carry out his plans of future punishment; and looking from the window, he watched if any one were lurking about, till he fancied that he detected figures stealing in and out among the trees, waiting to arrest him, and carry him off to take his stand by Angus, and be tried for his life.

Every moment was precious; and hastily securing his money, his jewels, and the contents of the casket he had given Margaret (but which he had hidden in a secure place to keep it concealed from her), he went along the passages and through the now deserted rooms, until he came to the bed-chamber, and stood at last near the old bay-window, close to which he had found his wife lying senseless on the floor on the night of Frederick Arkwright's supposed death.

Years and years gone by, his brother had stolen from his place of imprisonment into that very room, and into that same room his wife had crept through the same secret aperture, and had ultimately escaped. He could see that brother now, and starting at his own shadow thrown upon the wall, stepped back, fancying he saw his father and that brother's son as well, for the three appeared to come together and then vanish, leaving him trembling as before.

It was through that aperture he now proposed to go himself—to quit his father's house, and leave the curse that clung to it to fall on those who came to take possession in his stead. He had no care now for anything but life! and creeping on his hands and knees, found the space enlarge the farther he went, till he could almost stand upright, though he observed it narrowed afterwards, and at the bottom of a flight of steps discovered that it emerged into the outside room.

A faint streak of light coming through the

grated window enabled him to trace the outline
of that dismal room, but not to see the whole of
its contents; just enough to make it visible, yet
leave the darkened corners wrapped in shade;
gloomy and dull, and not to be pierced into by
his aching eyes. Then, full of associations connected with that room, and nervous now he stood
alone in it, he glanced fearfully about, and dreading some fresh calamity about to fall on him,
he advanced towards the door, but shrank back,
as he felt a man's arm stretched before him, and
barring his passage from the room.

He was in the act of making a sudden dash,
hoping to force his way, when a stern, harsh voice
startled him by saying—

"Not so fast, master, if you please. You and
I must have a little talk before you go, and as
there ain't much time to spare, why the sooner
it's got rid of the better."

"Angus!" cried Ellerton, breathless with astonishment.

"Yes, master; Angus. Or, if you like it better, your 'dog.' But a dog that has given over
whining, and come to show his teeth now you and
I ain't the friends we were, but must know a
something more of one another than we used
to do."

"How did you come here?"

17—2

"I don't know exactly how I came; but I managed it somehow, and as I wanted to see you, I crept in here as a likely place to hide in, and take my chance of finding you."

"Are you drunk or mad?"

"Neither, master, though I have had enough to make me, after what I have gone through. It's not pleasant, I can tell you, to be dragged through the streets, and hooted at, while you walk off like a gentleman, and leave me to take the consequences of what, by rights, you ought to take your share in. You haven't a man's heart, master, that's clear, or you'd have stood by me at a time I was in trouble, and not called me names to make me worse off than before."

"How did you get away?"

"Oh, I made a jump for it, and ran off as if I had fifty devils at my heels, instead of those two long-legged rascals that followed after and nearly caught me. But I dodged 'em, master— gave them the slip—and as I knew the ground, why I dodged and dodged, and left 'em looking for me where there was not much chance of finding me."

Ellerton had been taken by surprise, but he was now recovering himself. He dreaded Angus, and knew that his presence boded him no good. He had left him to suffer for his fault, and hoped he had got rid of him for ever, when, to his alarm, he saw him laying wait for him in his old quarters; and talking to him in a very different style from what he used to do.

But he was armed. He had taken the precaution to provide himself with a weapon in case of danger, and feeling in his breast to make sure that it was safe, he looked at Angus more calmly; but though he appeared to be less in dread of him, he spoke as if he did not wish to quarrel with him.

" I am glad you got away."

" I'm not so sure of that," said Angus. " It's my belief you'd have been better pleased if I was in the lock-up, or safe in gaol. But there's no fear of either just at present, now I have got my hands out of the handcuffs; and if they come, they wont get much for their pains—nor my old master either, if he plays any tricks, now I have come to tell him a bit of my mind, and have a talk with him."

The pale, faint streak had grown into a flood of light. The moon came shining through the iron bars, and Angus stood revealed in all his wretchedness, but in all his strength. His hands were bloody, his clothes torn and disordered, his hair straggling and wild, and his deportment so changed, he more resembled a hunted beast than a man ! The old obedience and awe of his master were gone. He had no fear of him now, but standing calmly and defiantly, he placed himself before the door, and looked at Ellerton as much as to say, that it was of no use trying to deceive him, for he knew him, and didn't mean to trust him again.

It would not do to grapple with him, or attempt to dash him to the ground, for Angus was on his guard; neither would it do to let him see he was afraid, for the moonlight shone on both their faces, and the least change would have been marked. He did not dare to let him see that he was armed, for Angus was armed as well, and holding his bill-hook in his hand, let the light glimpse on it as he held it half-raised and ready for a blow.

His own was the quicker weapon, but he did not wish, unless compelled, to use it, or fire, except in self-defence. But as Angus never moved, but stood as if expecting him to speak, he thought, that if he could only persuade him to listen to him, he might win him over to his old obedience, and get him to do as he desired.

"Angus," he said, " I am grieved that you should have suffered so much through me; but I never intended it, and am only sorry it has fallen out as it has. But it is not too late to mend matters. You may get off after all, and I shall only be too happy to reward you for what you have endured, if you will show me how it can be done."

"Reward!" cried Angus, almost fiercely; "and a pretty way you set about it, trying to send me out of the world like the black nigger I told you of, with the people looking at me, and screaming at me, as if I had been the devil incarnate. That's not a pleasant thing, you'll own, master; and I want to know how you would have liked it if you'd been treated as I was, and left in the lurch, after doing what I could to reward *you* for having saved my life?"

"A man can die but once," said Ellerton, fencing with the question.

"But not on a scaffold—not sent out of the world like a mad dog! And if it makes no difference to you, I should prefer dying a different kind of death, and when I am better prepared for it. To let you see I am in earnest, and mean to live as long as I can, just you look at this, which I picked up after those fellows had left, and after it had been kicked out of the way to prevent my getting it."

"You don't mean to say that you would use that dreadful thing again?" cried Ellerton, starting back and involuntarily shrinking from its sight.

"That depends upon circumstances," replied the other, "and how I may be used. It was about something of the sort I came to speak to you, so that I might make a clean breast of it and keep nothing back."

" Go on," said Ellerton, less inclined to believe in his man's peaceful intentions, and fully alive to the necessity of keeping a watchful eye on him.

" Well, then, you saved my life," Angus went on, " and as one good turn deserves another, I nearly saved your life just now, and might have been hanged for you, after you had put the thoughts of killing into my head, then called me a ruffian when I was frightened into telling of it."

" I can't keep here listening all night. Say what you have to say at once, or come some other time, for I can't stay now."

" But you must, master," said Angus, stepping before him. " I came on purpose to have a talk with you, and ain't half done yet. Besides, I may let you know a thing or two you will be glad to hear perhaps, and tell you more about old Daniel and what you wanted to know, than he could."

" Daniel !"

" He knew a something, but not so much as I do, of your brother and that rogue of a son of his you were so anxious about, in case he should turn up some day, and shoulder you out of the estate."

Ellerton looked at him, but said nothing.

The mention of his brother and his son put thoughts into his head he would not willingly have recalled, or have heard their names mentioned in that room after fancying that he had seen their shadows, and watched them melt away.

"I was sitting on the old log of a tree out yonder only this very morning, and looking at you know what, when a long-legged chap came up as said he knew me, and wanted to have a talk with me."

"Well?"

"Well, he spoke about things I did not understand, called me a gentleman, and said he had come to strike a bargain with me for making my fortune, and a lot of stuff of that sort as at first I could not make out; but I understood him fast enough when he went on, and said I had a right to the estate, and that if I liked I could take my sweetheart in my hand and turn you out."

"You?"

"Simple as I stand here. But he said so for all that; talked of documents (I think he called them), and wanted me to go before a lawyer and make an agreement with him."

"What for?" said Ellerton, more and more surprised.

"To pay him for his trouble in finding me out, so he said, and proving me to be—not

Angus Macleod, but Arthur Ellerton, the son of your brother, and the heir to what you thought you had a right to."

Had Angus seen the stealthy movement of his master's hand, or watched his heavy brow fall over his stern, cold eye, he might have paused a moment, and thought of what that movement meant, or why he looked at him so earnestly, and vainly tried to trace in the brutal, wild, and uncouth form before him, some resemblance to his brother.

"There is no knowing what I might have been tempted to do had he kept a civil tongue in his head, and not called you a lot of names," Angus went on. "For I *have* a sweetheart, master, and might have coaxed her into marrying me, had she been sure of being a squire's lady, and not the wife of a ' wretch' and ' rascal,' as you said I was, in the Court up yonder."

"A squire's lady?" said Ellerton, almost mocking him.

" So he said, and sure enough she might have been, only I did not quite like the idea of behaving ungrateful to you after what you had done for me. I could not bear the thought of that; and as I had sworn to be a faithful servant to you, I determined to keep my word, and, right or no right, let you keep where you was, and be my master, to the end of my days."

His eyes filled with tears as he said this, and even Ellerton, despite his coldness, appeared to be a little touched by this additional proof of his faithfulness and regard. Then changing suddenly when he thought that he, that abject and obedient slave, that Angus, whom he had picked out of the sea, should prove to be his nephew, and have it in his power to talk to him as his equal, if not his superior, he grew hard and stern again.

Angus knew nothing of this feeling working in his master's breast; but had he known it, it would have made no difference. He had come with a definite object, and was resolved to carry it out.

"Now, Uncle Mark," said he, "we stand on pretty equal terms; so let us rub out the slate and start a fresh score. You served your turn, and left me, as you thought, to pay your debt. But I'm here again, you see. My hands are at liberty, and now comes the bit of my mind I promised to tell you of before; as I said, I should bite. You called me a rascal, and now I am going to prove myself one. You gave me a taste for blood, and I like it so well, I mean to see how you will look chopped down by this, and if you will keep as quiet as the other did when lying at my feet. There ain't two pins to choose between you, and if the devil must have me, may as well be had for two as one, and be hanged for the pair of you."

Swing went the fatal bill-hook with a deadly aim. But before it fell, before he could bring it down, Ellerton fired and hit him. But a crashing blow succeeded—a deadly heavy blow, which struck down all before it, and felled the master at the servant's foot, as if he had been an ox killed in the shambles.

A long, deep, sighing groan, and all was still ! The light passed from the window ! The moon was hidden by a dense black cloud ! The stars were rayless, and darkness fell upon that awful place in which a man lay dead upon the floor; his blood flowing in a ghastly stream, and creeping under the door as if to follow the murderer in his flight, and track him as he went, limping, and slightly staggering, from the wound he had received.

CHAPTER XVI

CAUGHT IN A NOOSE.

Since the day when the "Green Dragon" first hung out its sign, nothing had equalled the stir and bustle taking place inside it at the present moment. All the best rooms were engaged; the servants had double work to do, the landlady and the landlord were in a state of unusual excitement, and the whole place in confusion, preparing for fresh arrivals.

Mrs. and Mr. Blissett (the latter fresh as a lark, and quite recovered of his accident) have just alighted from the mail. Mrs. Rushbrook has come down with them; the Reverend Mr. Arkwright is half asleep upon the sofa, Leonard and Bertha are engaged in a little private conversation, Frederick is assuring Mrs. Rushbrook of Margaret's safety, and the Captain standing in the centre of the apartment, recounting the particulars of what had happened to the whole assembly.

First, he had to narrate (although they had heard of it already) how Frederick had begged his brother to come down some time before, when

having borrowed a suit of his clothes and his card-
case, he had obtained an interview with Ellerton,
and passed himself on him in his stead. Next,
he told them with what ill-suppressed confusion
Ellerton had listened to the charges made
against him; delicately alluded to his having
challenged him, but spoke indignantly of the
other's cowardice; positively asserted that there
remained no doubt as to his guilt (he knew that
by his blustering), yet at the same time confessed
to the difficulty in bringing it home to him.
But as Margaret's safety had first to be assured,
he stated that they had been compelled to wait till
her husband could be enticed to leave his home
by some artifice, and Bertha be got into it—
when, aided by Jane, it was hoped that they might
devise some scheme for setting her at liberty, and
had fortunately succeeded.

Mrs. Rushbrook did not know what to do, but
bursting into tears, she assured Frederick of her
gratitude, regretting that he had not been her
son-in-law instead of the monster her daughter had
accepted, and wished, for her part, that he had
been hanged, drawn, and quartered, before she
had set eyes on him. But when she heard that
a daughter of hers had been assisted by low
gipsy women, and sheltered in one of their nasty
tents, she was a little out of temper, and might

have burst into another fit of crying, had she not heard that Margaret was already in the house, and fast recovering from the shock upon her nervous system; then flying upstairs she fell almost fainting on her bed, and fondling and embracing her, begged of her to forgive her for having persuaded her to marry against her inclination, and sacrifice herself to please her.

But on the news arriving that Angus had escaped, a fresh scene ensued. Ellerton would now be free to act as he pleased, and relieved of all fear from his servant's accusation, might endeavour to get his wife back into his power, unless they placed her beyond his reach, or could protect her from his violence. On hearing which, the Captain volunteered to mount guard at her door and keep off trespassers; scare them by his very sight, and thrash a whole host of them, if they so much as showed themselves while he stood sentinel over the fair one entrusted to his charge.

But, as nothing occurred to challenge his bravery, and as the night passed away in quiet, Frederick and the Captain agreed to go into the town and inquire further into the matter—when they saw the Northumbrian coming towards them, running at full speed, his cap off, his long skirts flying behind him, and his big feet pounding the road as if they had been a couple of pavior's hammers.

"What is the matter?" asked Frederick, as soon as he came within speaking distance.

"The matter!" gasped Mr. Bostock. "Why death an' destruction are the matter, an' the most awfu' piece of business that has taken place sin' the days o' Cain." Speaking in short sentences, blowing out his cheeks, and fanning himself with his coat-tails, Mr. Bostock stood to recover his breath, and then went on. "It's no so easy to explain it just the noo, though it's my belief that fellow Angus has done it on purpose to cheat me, and killed his master—as he ca'd him—out of revenge."

"You don't mean to say that Mr. Ellerton is dead?" cried Frederick.

"Yes, but I do though. But the whole affair is so awfu', and my stomach that faint, unless you gi' me a drap o' brandy, or whisky, to steady my nerves, I shall collapse, an' fall down flat as a pancake."

As he really seemed to require something, Frederick ordered him a dram; and thus refreshed, Mr. Bostock offered to accompany them upstairs and tell the particulars of what he had seen to the assembled company.

He had, as it appeared, been sadly put out on

finding that Angus had been committed for trial, and getting up early the following morning, went to see if he could get to speak with Mr. Ellerton, and sell him his secret at a moderate price. But as no one came to answer his ringing, he took the liberty to walk round the house, thinking to find some one, when he came to where an old porch-way, and a room built just outside, afforded him, as he thought, a chance.

No one was to be seen there, or anywhere else, and the deathly stillness of the place made him feel so uncomfortable that he was making off, when he saw a something which attracted his attention, and looking closer, discovered that it was a streak of blood.

Big fellow as he was, and used to treat things roughly, the sight of blood, as he said, always turned him sick, and he was about going away, when, tempted by his curiosity, he pushed the door a little way open, and saw to his horror, a man lying dead upon the floor, and all the signs of a brutal murder having been committed.

Frightened out of his wits in case any one should come and take him up upon suspicion, he had just time to catch a glimpse of the face, then tucking up his skirts, took to his heels and ran!—ran till he saw the Captain and his friend, and then resolved to tell them what he had seen, and leave them to act as they thought proper.

The news soon spread, and on inquiry it appeared that an exploded pistol had been discovered by the dead man's side, and a track of blood leading from the doorway to the fields, tending to the supposition that the murderer had been wounded, either before or after his attack, and that he could not long elude pursuit.

Mr. Bostock hereupon beckoned mysteriously to Leonard, and, begging a few minutes' private conversation, informed him that if he would only reward him liberally he would convince him that he was the sole surviving heir to the Ellerton estate, and the legitimate claimant, now his brother Angus was as good as gone, to all his possessions.

To his surprise, Leonard did not express the gratitude he expected, nor fall upon his neck and call him his benefactor. He rather seemed to make light of the whole affair, and startled Mr. Bostock by saying—

" Oh, yes. You told me something of that before, but not the full particulars. You had somebody else in your eye then, who, you thought, would pay you better, and do more for you than I should—that poor wretch Angus, who has now to answer to the law for his offence ; and my claim, if I choose to enforce it, does not admit of dispute."

" Eigh, but you canna do it without my help. It's no so easy as you think to establish your rights without consulting me; an' unless you pay me weel I'll go back to Alnwick, tie a stane to my documents, an' pitch 'em into the Tyne like a dog that's o'er bad wi' the distemper."

" The fact is," said Mr. Blissett, stepping between them, " Poll Woodruff—I beg her pardon, Mrs. Savaker—has been beforehand with you. She is dead, poor woman, but before she died, she acknowledged Leonard to be her son, and the identical boy she turned over to be adopted by me at a time that she was glad to get rid of him on any terms. Her natural feelings came back to her when on her death-bed, and so you see———"

" Only to think of that noo! Eigh, but she's a bad un, an' always were, an' will meet wi' her deserts in the place she's gane te, or I'm much mistaken," said Mr. Bostock, with a sudden drop of his features.

" Be good enough to hear me out," resumed Mr. Blissett. " Having heard of the breakdown of that abominable long-stage coach, and of the

accident that followed, she ascertained my address
from the people at the inn where I was laid up;
instructed her lawyer to come to me when she
found herself seriously ill in consequence of
bursting a blood-vessel in a fit of passion, and
authorized him to state that Leonard Blissett,
my adopted son, was her son, and the second son
by her marriage with Reuben Craddock, otherwise Arthur Ellerton."

" An' do you mean to say that that spitfire,
Poll, has had the audacity to swindle me in that
way?" cried the Northumbrian, now in a towering passion.

" You will be good enough to remember that
Mrs. Savaker was my mother," said Leonard,
" and though a little hasty in her temper, by no
means a badly disposed woman."

" A wild cat war a fool to her, an' as to her
tongue, a' the brass instruments blawing together
could no mack such a clang as she could if you
only put her out. There war no peace wi' her on
earth, an' now she's dead, if the deil don't send
her back again, he's far more guod-natured than
I tack him to be."

Disgusted at the treatment he had received,
Mr. Bostock went grumbling out of the room,
and lumbering downstairs, stood for a moment at
the door-step; then cursing his ill-luck, he went

grumbling off, and made up his mind to make his brother stand in for his share of the expenses, or the whole of them, for putting him on a wrong scent, and wasting his time on a wild-goose chase.

Mr. Bostock got rid of, the next thought was Angus, and what had become of him—whether he had intentionally killed Mr. Ellerton, or had struck him down in self-defence. The river had been dragged, every conceivable place searched, and yet no sign of him : so that it came to be believed that he was either far away, or was skulking in some corner close at hand, and might, after all, elude pursuit, unless his wound proved fatal.

Expectation was at its height, and various guesses were set afoot regarding his whereabouts, when the news arrived that he had been discovered, and close in the neighbourhood.

He had been found. But how ? Not skulking in a corner or hiding in a ditch, but dead and hanging from a branch of a tree; and so completely hidden by the leaves, that if an accident had not revealed him, he would have remained unnoticed for some time to come.

The grass was torn and trampled about the tree, leading to the supposition that some foul play had taken place ; and though at first it had been suggested that Angus had committed suicide, the evidence of the trampled grass, and the general appearance of the place, altered that view, and left no doubt that the two gipsies who had followed him had overpowered and lynched him for killing one of their companions.

CHAPTER XVII.

AS IT SHOULD BE.

In those same meadows where, two years before, Frederick had had the good fortune to rescue Margaret from her unromantic adventure with the cow, and where she had lost her heart, a pair of lovers might be seen walking arm-in-arm, listening to the vows they had uttered for the thousandth time, and prepared to endure torments unutterable rather than break.

Springtime had come again, and lightly stepping on the grass, that happy pair appeared to be recalling the past as they pointed to the stile, the hedgerow, and that particular part of it behind which Margaret had disappeared while he had stood to wave his hand, wishing he dared to follow her. There was no aunt now to be afraid of; no screeching and no scolding to endure, but all were calmness and content. The love she had felt in secret then, she dared to speak of boldly now, and openly declare her passion unabated for the adventurous youth who had first attracted her, and won her by a smile.

The misery that had befallen her since the

time when stealing out of doors she had left her aunt asleep, only to get a peep at Frederick, and watch him through the hedge, had passed like a disordered dream! She remembered, yet hated to remember; while the least allusion to that fatal night, on which she had seen, as she imagined, her lover killed, served but to increase her agony, and throw her back into her old distraction.

Time, it was said, would cure all this, and restore her to herself—the sooner if she could be brought in contact with the scenes of her former delight, and have a daily opportunity of roaming in the fields where she had met with Frederick. And so it proved. The calmness of her present life, its freedom from excitement, and the consciousness gradually dawning upon her of what had really happened, tended slowly but surely to confirm her health, and remove the evil consequences of her past derangement.

Trusting to such natural agencies as had been suggested to bring her back to reason, it had been arranged that she should take up her abode, not at her aunt's, but with Frederick's family for a time, and though Miss Hindmarsh was, of course, indignant at the preference shown to the Arkwrights, she did not think it policy to come to an open rupture with her niece; but swallowed her indignation, and keeping it in store, promised herself to repay the slight at the first possible opportunity.

It was certainly very tantalizing to see them walking arm-in-arm as she sat at her bedroom window and watched them strolling up and down, or sitting in the shade, and playing the parts of lovers to perfection ! She had no beau now, no arm to hang upon, and not the remotest chance of finding one, now that the Captain had proved unfaithful, and strutted past her window without taking the slightest notice of her. Yet, looking from her window, and seeing Frederick's arm steal round his dear one's waist, she could not help thinking that once upon a time she had been embraced herself, and flattered with the hope of one day becoming Mrs. Captain Conroy Nubbleton !

Did her eyes deceive her, or was that her Conroy flourishing his stick, and making signs to her? He was doing something of the sort, but as she could not make him out distinctly without spectacles, she ran to fetch them, and on coming back, had the mortification to see him beckoning, not to her, but to her niece and Frederick ! beckoning them to go in to breakfast, and making himself conspicuous in so marked a manner that she was agonized to see him ; standing on the top of a bank in danger of falling, and flourishing his little cane like a conductor beating time to an orchestra.

At length, and after beckoning and shouting for some time longer, he succeeded in attracting their attention, then turned away; but on glancing back to make sure that they were following, he happened to see Miss Hindmarsh at the window, and twisting on his heel left her, either leaning out, or tumbling out, he did not much care which.

As to the breakfast, they had to get it how they could, for, during their absence, a letter had arrived announcing the rector's dangerous illness, and expressing a wish that Mr. Ark-wright, or the Reverend Mr. Ernest, should immediately go down to Yorkshire and close his eyes. Ernest was of course anxious to start at once, and though there had been some little trouble in getting him up, and in getting him ready, he was dressed at last, and swallowing a a cup of scalding tea as fast as he could.

The pony-chaise was at the door, the portmanteau packed and inside, and all things but the reverend gentleman ready for a start. At length, and after his mother had told him a dozen times he would be too late, and that the coach would be sure to be gone, he jumped into the chaise, bid his mother good-bye, and on her begging and requesting him to write the moment he arrived, and let her know about her dear good brother (she was sobbing very badly), Ernest said, " All right," started off at a gallop, and by good luck caught the coach just as it was starting; when he stepped into it, ate the remainder of his breakfast between the stages, then snuggling his head in a corner, stretched out his legs, and slept the remainder of the way.

At the end of two days a letter came to say that his uncle was dead; that he had arrived just in time to give him the benefit of his consolation, and had the satisfaction of seeing the good old man die as a Christian should. Not like the old vagabond who had cut him off with a shilling, but impressed with a sense of what was due to him; for he had not only left him his heir, but had made a touching appeal to the Bishop to interest himself in his (Ernest's) behalf, and use his best endeavours to confer on him the rectorship left vacant by his death.

Fortunate nephews! May they cherish their uncles' memories, and be grateful to them for their goodness! May they drink port wine in moderation; be content with one plateful of turtle, and not go asking for more, but live to be examples of abstemiousness and sobriety! May they—but as one of them is shortly to be married we will leave him in his wife's care, and recommend the other to get married as soon as possible —to keep his eyes open and look about for a suitable partner.

First Frederick, then Leonard, and now the Reverend Mr. Arkwright! All three had benefited when they least expected it, and been enriched to their hearts' content; the brothers by their uncles, and Leonard, through his right to the Ellerton estate, come into his possession by the death of one he might not have liked to call his brother, or look upon as an equal, had he lived.

But as Bertha said she could not bear the place, and should never be able to sleep a wink in it after what had happened, it was decided to sell the estate and purchase another, where Margaret could come and stay with them and be happy, which it could not be expected she would be in the old house—to be always reminded of her misery, or see her husband's ghost, or Angus's, stalking about in the dead of night, and frightening her out of her wits! Her mother too. But then her mother preferred living by herself; at least she said so, and as a nice little cottage could easily be got not very far off, where they could see her daily, and be quite, or more comfortable, than if she lived with them, (which Bertha did not intend she should,) it was the thing of all others to make them as happy as they could be.

But there was one person they had forgotten, and that was Mr. Bostock.

He had borne his disappointment much after the way that an eel bears skinning. He had twirled and twisted, done all he could to avoid it, but submitted when he found that he could not help it. He had lost his money! He had lost chance after chance, and found himself left in the lurch, to his intense disgust. His brother threw the whole blame of failure on him, and snapped his fingers in his face when he talked of making him stand half the expense; bullied him for asking, and, like a true Northumbrian, declined to part with his brass unless he saw something to be got by it; so that Mr. Bostock had nothing left for it but patience, and a shuffling of the cards in hopes to turn up trumps.

The first thing that comforted him, was his seeing an advertisement announcing the sale of the Ellerton estate, when up he came by the long-stage coach, and as he passed by the "Castle" at Newark, he shook his fist at its closed shutters, and swearing at its late proprietress as the cause of all his troubles, wished her—where, it is not necessary to mention.

The business he had come upon was arranged

sooner than he expected, and might have been settled before, had he been less exorbitant in his demands. Feeling that some compensation was due to him for the trouble he had taken in discovering Angus, and that Mrs. Savaker had been traced to the inn at Newark through him, it was thought that by granting him a long lease of the " Castle," at a nominal rent, and by making him a present of its contents, that he would be paid handsomely, and have an opportunity of convincing people, by his own moderate charges, what an exorbitant set innkeepers were, and how monstrously they overcharged their unfortunate customers.

Mr. Bostock was satisfied, and on taking possession, duly installed himself in the little bar-parlour, where he cut down the exciseman and hung himself up in his place. His portrait was a success, his drab great-coat true to nature, and the imperishable garment perfect even to the button-holes; reflecting the greatest credit on the ingenious artist who had painted it, after he had finished touching up the sign-board, and at the small charge of thirty shillings.

Mr. Bostock was not popular. He overcharged abominably: bought at the cheapest and sold at the dearest, starved his servants, and disgusted his customers, and in less than a year had brought the " Castle" so low, he was glad to get rid of the lease and fittings for a good round sum ; and settling down at Black Acre Farm, —lately left him by his uncle—was never known to travel South, or risk an innkeeper's imposition afterwards, for he had practised it himself, and knew by experience the exorbitant profits they got.

Without troubling themselves concerning him, what he did, or where he went, our old familiar friends drew closer together in a family circle, and left him to his fate. Mr. and Mrs. Blissett, the happiest of couples, the best-natured and the most anxious to please ; while Leonard, although not a son by blood, proved himself deserving of the affection and regard of those who had protected him in his need, and rescued him from a fate fearful to contemplate.

The other parties interested in this remarkably faithful, most true, and particular narrative, deserve equally to be remembered ; but as an unusually fine autumn had now set in, and as it was the best time of the year for a continental tour, it was arranged for the brace of marriages to take place without delay—Margaret and Frederick, Bertha and Leonard—and as the principals were agreed, and as no one had a word to say against it, why of course the question was carried unanimously, and preparations for the double wedding pushed forward without delay.

Two excellent estates having been found exactly suiting them, and so close together that they seemed as if they had been made on purpose, Bertha expressed herself enraptured, and as Margaret was happy and contented with anything, and as there was the prettiest church, the prettiest village, magnificent woods, green fields, and a noble river close at hand, they must have been very hard to please had they not been satisfied, and delighted with the spot they had chosen.

That village church is soon to witness a four-fold happiness, and the village itself to be a scene of great rejoicing; for a grand feast has been prepared and a general holiday agreed upon, to celebrate the weddings which are to take place— as soon as the clergyman, the brides and bride-grooms make their appearance.

Margaret is dressed for a second bridal. There is no sadness at her heart now, and no regret to interrupt her happiness, as she looks at herself in the glass, and says, that Jane has dressed her to perfection. But Jane replies that she has had very little to do with it, and declares that her mistress can't help looking well, dress how she will, and gets scolded because she vows that she never saw her look half so beautiful before.

But as this scolding is accompanied by a smile, and a fresh look in the glass, Jane doesn't care much about it, but pins on the last bow exactly where it should be, and shakes out the veil to make it fall down gracefully.

But as that prettiest of all churches has yet to be reached, and as Frederick will be growing impatient, Margaret prepares to join Bertha—who has been ready ever so long, and is coming to look for her—when the two sisters compare notes, and turn one another about to make sure that everything is as it should be, when they step into the carriage, and on alighting, have the satisfaction to see the Captain waiting for them in the porch, smiling and kissing his one finger, and looking for all the world as if he had been a big boy out for a holiday.

But as it is time to be serious, and as the two Miss Blissetts are the bridesmaids, and are looking, as bridesmaids always look—as if they wished to change places with the brides and represent them at the shortest notice—the ladies step up the aisle, and meet the gentlemen at the other end, where they have been waiting for the last half hour.

The ceremony over, and the bells set ringing, the happy train wends its way back again ; the brides with their husbands, the bridesmaids, the

Captain, Mrs. Rushbrook, and Mr. and Mrs. Blissett, with the clergyman, bringing up the rear.

The wedding-breakfast is perfect in its way; and though Mrs. Rusnbrook looks a little melancholy, and talks of the uncertainty of human happiness, the Captain maintains the contrary, and gets rather fuddled by taking wine with everybody, and wishing everybody as happy as himself. And, as the Captain was great at making a speech, and as he was the proper person to propose the healths of the brides and bridegrooms (at least, he thought he was), he rose, and looking about him with the grandest, but at the same time the most affable expression, commenced his oration.

He started tolerably well; and speaking of the blessings which he hoped they might enjoy, and of the happiness awaiting them, grew flowery and pathetic; but as one of the Miss Blissetts began crying (as bridesmaids will) he grew nervous, and beginning to sniff and cough, had to slap his little chest to renew his courage, then falling back on military similes (as captains will), he compared the brides to a couple of fortresses taken after a desperate attack, and the bridegrooms to two courageous lions that it was no good trying to resist. But when he spoke of Frederick, called him his dear friend, and associated his name with Margaret's, he broke down again, then, struggling with his feelings, tried to gulp his tears; but getting worse and worse, he buried his face in his hands, and sank back in his chair unable to say another word.

His campaigning is over; he has given up all thoughts of promotion, and devoted himself to Frederick for the remainder of his life. He is no longer tutor. He is the friend and companion of his dearly-loved pupil; but trusts to live to be drill-sergeant to any little recruits that may arrive, and put them through their facings. Let us hope they may, and that the gallant Captain may still continue at his post for many a year to come, a soldier and a gentleman; and, though neglected by his country, ready to step forward to her rescue, and, by God's blessing, do his part in defending her against all comers, should they ever try to come.

Margaret's happiness is now complete. Her sufferings may not be spoken of, nor her first husband mentioned for fear of recalling her affliction. It is with the future we have now to deal, not with the past; with her contentment, not her misery. May all good thoughts attend her, and may she and her sister and their husbands, find the promised joys in married life people generally find whose tempers assimilate, and where a desire to please animates both parties.

THE END.